JUN 0 6 2013

NINE DAYS

NINE DAYS

fred hiatt

delacorte press

Text copyright © 2013 by Fred Hiatt
Jacket art copyright © 2013 by Debra Lill
Afterword copyright © 2013 by Ti-Anna Wang

All rights reserved. Published in the United States by Delacorte Press, an imprint of Random House Children's Books, a division of Random House, Inc., New York.

Delacorte Press is a registered trademark and the colophon is a trademark of Random House, Inc.

Visit us on the Web! randomhouse.com/teens
Educators and librarians, for a variety of teaching tools, visit us at RHTeachersLibrarians.com

Library of Congress Cataloging-in-Publication Data
Hiatt, Fred.
Nine days / Fred Hiatt. — 1st ed.
p. cm.
Summary: Tenth-graders Ethan and Ti-Anna go to Hong Kong seeking her father, an exiled Chinese democracy activist who has disappeared, and follow his trail to Vietnam and back, also uncovering illegal activity along the way. Includes author's note and the history behind the novel written by the girl who inspired it.—provided by publisher
ISBN 978-0-385-74273-3 (trade hardcover) — ISBN 978-0-375-99073-1 (glb) — ISBN 978-0-307-97727-4 (ebook) [1. Missing persons—Fiction. 2. Voyages and travels—Fiction. 3. Dissenters—Fiction. 4. Human trafficking—Fiction. 5. Chinese Americans—Fiction. 6. Hong Kong (China)—Fiction. 7. Vietnam—Fiction. 8. Maryland—Fiction.] I. Title.
PZ7.H495Nin 2013
[Fic]—dc23
2012008653

The text of this book is set in 12-point Goudy.
Book design by Kenny Holcomb

Printed in the United States of America
10 9 8 7 6 5 4 3 2 1
First Edition

To Nate

Prologue

Monday, July 30, 9:15 a.m. (EDT)
Just outside Washington, D.C.

Already the summer heat is defeating the wheezing air-conditioning unit in a third-floor bedroom window of an apartment in Bethesda, Maryland.

A fifteen-year-old girl in a T-shirt and shorts kicks off her sheet, rises and slips into the chair in front of her computer. While it boots up, she listens to make sure her mother is paying no attention. Tucking her long black hair behind one ear, she opens a document that a friend sent her sometime during the night.

It begins: `When Ti-Anna's father disappeared . . .`

She reads on.

Rockville, Maryland

Seven miles to the north, a juvenile court judge enters the office behind her courtroom, slings her briefcase onto her desk, sets down her coffee and powers up her desktop.

Scrolling through the weekend's accumulation of email, she

comes across a document in an attachment, with only a brief accompanying note. She sighs when she notes its length. She has other paperwork she should be doing. On Mondays she does not begin hearing cases until after noon.

But curiosity gets the better of her. Sipping her coffee through the plastic top, she clicks open the attachment.

Beijing, China

Halfway around the world, in a windowless, over-air-conditioned office deep in the intelligence agency headquarters of the People's Republic of China, it is already Monday night.

A middle-aged man with gray-flecked hair and his necktie tucked into his shirt (a habit whenever he drinks tea) has set a printout of the same document on the metal desk before him. In fact, he has aligned two copies: one in English and, slightly off to the side, one that has been translated into Mandarin by the agency's computers.

Because the computer routinely assigns the first few words of any document as its title, atop every page of the English edition is printed: `WhenTi-Anna'sfatherdisappeared.doc`.

With a heavy sigh, he too begins to read.

Chapter 1

When Ti-Anna's father disappeared, it wasn't one of those sudden things. I didn't see him get blown off a cliff or conked on the head and bundled into a windowless van. But he disappeared just the same, and Ti-Anna and I decided we had to do something about it.

It may seem, by the time I finish telling what happened, that that wasn't the brightest decision. I ended up traveling halfway around the world without telling my parents. I nearly killed someone, and nearly got myself and my best friend killed too. And while we may not exactly have failed, we certainly didn't accomplish what we set out to accomplish.

But every step of the way, it felt like I was doing the right thing, until we were in so deep that I wasn't thinking anymore whether it was the right thing or not. I was just trying to survive, along with Ti-Anna.

Now my parents and the judge think I should be remorseful. I have to write how sorry I am, and if I'm not, I guess the judge could send me away.

So I know I should just write *Yes, I am remorseful*. How hard could that be?

But as I think about it all, I'm feeling a lot of different things. Of course I'm not delighted to have a cast on my leg. I'm remorseful about that. I wish I didn't owe my parents so much money. And there's definitely a lot I did along the way that I'm not proud of.

But can I honestly say I wouldn't do it again? I don't know. I really don't.

So I'm going to write what happened, exactly as it happened, to the best of my honest recollection, from the very beginning, whether or not it looks good to the judge or anyone else.

When I'm done, maybe I'll go back and stick in a lot of sorrys and take out a bunch of truth.

And maybe I won't. I believe in the truth, maybe too much sometimes. In a way, that was how this whole thing started.

Chapter 2

Beginning at the beginning means taking you back to school—
to Mr. Stoltz's sleepy tenth-grade world history class, to be specific.
I *am* remorseful about that. I apologize.

That's where the story begins.

It was one of those groggy Washington afternoons in early May
when just about everyone is staring at the clock and willing the
buzzer to sound so they can get out of school.

I got into an argument about Mao Zedong.

Don't jump to the conclusion that I'm a total nerd. I am not. I'm
reasonably coordinated. I'm not terrible to look at. Maybe I'm not
the most social kid in the world, but I have friends.

It is true that I don't mind spending time by myself. I have two
parents who love me, but they're both absentminded physicists who
are away at conferences a lot of the time. They had two kids, and
then a long time after that they had me, and sometimes I think it
slips their minds that there's a third kid in the family.

Of course, my mother would deny that she's absentminded
and say that my saying she's absentminded just proves I'm not a

good observer. Which I would say proves how absentminded she really is.

My older brother and sister love me, but they don't live at home anymore. So over the years I've learned to entertain myself. I love to draw, and to read. I've dived into Greek mythology. Ancient writing systems. Aztec religion. Medieval war machines. Code-breaking during World War II.

And China. I wouldn't call China a phase. I've been reading about China for a long time, and the more I learn, the more I want to know.

So when Mr. Stoltz called Mao "the father of his nation," the George Washington of modern China, it set me off.

On certain subjects I feel strongly, and sometimes when I hear something dumb, or wrong, I can't stop myself.

This was one of those times.

I raised my hand.

Mr. Stoltz sighed.

"Yes, Ethan?"

I said I didn't recall that George Washington ever caused a famine that killed twenty million of his countrymen.

To which one of my classmates, a boy with expensive sunglasses whose father is a diplomat in the Chinese embassy, said I was being culturally insensitive, because Chinese people were proud of Mao and what he'd done for their country. Mao had brought China from the dark ages into the modern world, he said, and who was I to go against the Chinese people?

At that point I should have apologized and said I respect their point of view.

Instead I chose to inquire what kind of father would make his nation take a "Great Leap Forward" in which impoverished peasants had to turn their backyards into iron factories and melt down

6

their pots and pans so that before you knew it no one could cook dinner anymore.

And because that worked out so well, he tried something even crazier a couple of decades later (that's right; no term limits in Communist China), which he called the Cultural Revolution. That involved getting young people to turn against their parents and even beat them, and punishing anyone who had any formal education.

I wasn't quite as diplomatic as I might have been. Certainly it was more than Mr. Stoltz had bargained for. I'm sure he knew I was right; he knew what had happened in China during the Cultural Revolution.

But instead of backing me up, he just tried to calm us all down with a little sermon about different perspectives on history, and how we all need to be open to each other's points of view.

When the bell rang, the diplomat's son glared at me as he walked out, with a couple of his buddies following him and glaring too. That would have been the end of it if Ti-Anna hadn't waited until everyone else had left the classroom and then come over to talk to me.

I didn't even notice her at first. I was staring at my desk, letting the blood drain from my face. She must have been standing there for a couple of minutes before I looked up.

To say I was surprised would be an understatement. I'd known Ti-Anna since sixth grade, and of course I knew some basic facts about her, like you do if you've been in classes with someone. That her parents came from China, but that she didn't hang out much with the other Chinese students. That she was smart but quiet, and hardly ever talked in class. And, yes, that she was, as they used to say in the old detective novels, easy on the eyes.

But if she had said a dozen words to me in the five years we'd been classmates, I couldn't remember more than eleven of them.

So I was surprised to see her there, and even more surprised when she said, in her quiet voice, "Thank you, Ethan."

"For what?"

"For being brave enough to say those things about Mao. Some Chinese people think that to be patriotic they can't be honest about their country. I think the opposite. And every single thing you said was one hundred percent true."

Then she tucked her hair behind her ear, smiled a dazzling smile and added, "Even if I might not have phrased them in exactly the same way." And walked out of the classroom.

I spent the rest of the day, and a good part of the night, thinking about her.

Chapter 3

At my school you can leave at lunchtime, and most kids do. They go in groups and gaggles to fast-food places or to the deli on the corner. I usually bring a peanut butter sandwich and find a quiet spot to read. Ti-Anna usually brings lunch too, because her family doesn't have much money, though of course I didn't know that at first. Sometimes she sat in the cafeteria with her friends, but I had noticed that sometimes she ate by herself, in the same general area as me—out on the bleachers overlooking the track.

So the day after she talked to me in class, I waited until I thought she might be out there, and then I walked out and acted surprised to see her. I sat on the bench just above hers, and we started to talk. The next day we went out at about the same time and sat on the same bench, and we did that pretty much every day until finals, except when it rained.

After a few days, I started finding her when school ended, and I'd walk my bike alongside her while she walked home, a mile or so from school. We'd talk outside her apartment building. She never asked me in, and I never asked to go in. I got to know the bench in front of her building pretty well.

When I think back to our talks, of course the one I remember best is the day she told me her father had disappeared. But by then, we'd done a lot of talking—about her father, yes, because she was really proud of him, but about a lot of other things too. Ti-Anna didn't like to talk about herself, but it turned out we had a lot in common, even though we were really different. Or we were really different in similar ways.

For example: my parents believe that if you are born intelligent, the only reasonable course of action is to become a scientist. They wouldn't admit that, certainly not to me, but there it is.

And that's a problem, because my big brother is a physics whiz, like they are, and my sister is probably going to win a Nobel Prize in chemistry by the time she's thirty.

Whereas I've never once had a lab come out the way the teacher said it should. What I love is to read history, biographies, human rights reports. My parents pretend to think that's fine too, when they notice. But they don't really get it.

Ti-Anna was always two steps ahead of the lab teacher's directions, but her parents didn't really approve of her love of science. They're both from China. Ti-Anna was born there too, but her family came to America when she was four, so she sounds totally American. Her father, as she explained to me one lunchtime while we watched the cheerleading team practice, was a big deal in the Chinese democracy movement.

"Wait—Chen Jie-min—that's your father?" I asked.

"You've heard of him?"

"Of course!" I said. "Wow. I had no idea."

She looked pleased and a little surprised. But if you know anything about China today, you've heard of Ti-Anna's father.

"But a man like him—I mean—I wouldn't think he'd have anything against girls becoming scientists."

"Oh, it's not that," Ti-Anna said. "It's more—it's hard to explain." She took a bite of her apple. "Ever since we came to America, he thinks about nothing except going back and helping China become a democracy. That's his whole life, and it's my mother's life—typing his articles and letters, helping answer his mail, whatever needs doing. They think it should be my life too."

She stopped, and I thought that was the end of it. The cheerleaders had collapsed in a laughing heap, and Ti-Anna seemed to be studying them as they untangled themselves.

But she continued. "Being good at science, and getting into a good college, and becoming a biochemist in the United States—for him, that would be a waste, something that a million other kids could do, that a million other Chinese immigrant kids *will* do. For them, there's nothing wrong with it. For me, it would be abandoning the cause he's given his life to," she said. "And that I should be giving my life to also. Just look at my name."

"What about your name?" I asked. A little unusual, maybe, but I said I was sure there were American biochemists with odder ones.

"The 'Ti' in Ti-Anna?" she answered. "In Chinese, it's the same character as in 'Tiananmen.'"

She knew that I'd recognize that word. Tiananmen is the giant square in the heart of Beijing where thousands of young Chinese gathered the last time there was open protest in China—way back in 1989—demanding more freedom. They put up a big replica of the Statue of Liberty, but in the end Chinese soldiers broke up the demonstration by killing a lot of protesters and putting a lot more of them in jail.

Including Ti-Anna's father.

"So I'm named for a movement, and for the martyrs to freedom, and for my dad's cause." She sighed. "How could I grow up to be a postdoc in a lab at the University of Maryland?"

Chapter 4

One afternoon as we rounded the corner to her apartment building, Ti-Anna shuddered as if she'd just sucked on a lemon. She whispered for me to look at a blue Taurus parked across from her front entrance.

"It's *them*," she said. "From the embassy."

"What for?"

"Who knows?" she said. "Sometimes they sit there for hours. Keeping track of who my father meets with, maybe. Or trying to intimidate him." She studied the car with disgust. "Good luck with that."

She said good-bye and went inside; I eventually realized that she never lingered when the Taurus was there.

On afternoons when it wasn't there, though, she'd happily talk until close to suppertime, though it was hot, and not the most comfortable place. A lot of the time, we talked about China. She'd never been back, and her memories were fragmentary but vivid, she told me.

She could close her eyes and feel the padding as she clutched her mother's jacket, her mother bicycling through a freezing Beijing morning with Ti-Anna perched behind. She could remember the cracks in the beige paint on the wall beside her bed, in the room she'd shared with her grandmother. She thought she could still hear police hammering on the apartment door when they took her father away one night, though her mother insisted she'd been fast asleep and couldn't possibly remember.

Sometimes, she said, a smell from a diesel truck, or a restaurant exhaust fan, or something she couldn't even trace, would carry her back with dizzying force.

"Though I know it's changed completely since my parents left," she said. "It was crazy in the old days, like you were saying about Mao. But it's not like that now."

Her parents sometimes talked about what it was like when they were her age, and you couldn't do anything without Communist Party permission. The Party decided whom you could marry, where you could live, whether you'd go to college or spend your life growing rice. You could wear any color you wanted, as long as it was drab gray or faded blue.

Now the government pretty much left people alone. They could marry, get rich, stay poor, buy or sell their apartments, dress as they pleased.

The one thing they couldn't do—and here's where her father came in—was say anything bad about the Party, or suggest that maybe other people should have a chance at running the country.

"The Communists are stubborn, but my dad is as stubborn as they are," Ti-Anna said. "He spent four years in prison for believing in democracy. Came out, wrote another letter for democracy, and went right back in. They only let him out again after he promised to leave the country. For my sake, and my mother's, he promised, but he hated to do it. He's sure he'll go back one day."

"And what do you think?"

Ti-Anna didn't answer right away.

"I think he's the bravest man you could imagine, and I think everything he says about what China needs is right," she said finally. "But I'm not sure so many people in China are interested in hearing about it right now, since in so many ways their lives have improved."

Just then a small, gray-haired woman got off the bus that stopped by the apartment building. Ti-Anna bolted off the bench.

"Pretend you don't know me," she said.

At first I thought I must have heard wrong. But she strode away, toward her mother—because of course that's who it was—and I bent down, pretending to fix my gears.

As they passed, I heard them talking in Chinese. I looked up in time to see Ti-Anna open the door for her mother, who was about a foot shorter than Ti-Anna and was carrying a cloth shopping bag. Then they were gone, and it was suddenly very quiet on the sidewalk.

I waited by my bike for—well, for a long time. I was sure Ti-Anna would come out and apologize, or at least explain what was so repugnant about me that she had to pretend I was a stranger. But she didn't come out, and she didn't come out, and eventually I got nervous that some other tenant would wonder why this curly-haired kid was loitering outside the apartment building.

So I shouldered my backpack and wheeled away.

Chapter 5

That was a Friday, so I had the whole weekend to stew. At lunch-time on Monday I chose a bench down toward the practice football field, away from where we usually sat. After about ten minutes, I heard someone behind me.

"Sorry," she said as she sat down next to me. She looked at me as though she meant it, and just like that I wasn't mad anymore. I shrugged, as if to say, no big deal.

"Your mom doesn't approve of boys?" I asked.

"American boys," she said. "Or American girls, for that matter. Like I told you, being in America is just a temporary and unfortu-nate condition, as far as my parents are concerned. Anything that might distract us—anything that might get us more connected to life here—is a bad thing."

"But you have friends," I said. "You're always hanging out with Janice Twersky, right?"

"Janice has been my best friend since forever," Ti-Anna agreed. "My parents like her and her family, and on one level they under-stand that every child has to have friends.

"But—well, pretty much the only people they talk to are other exiles in the democracy movement. Or people who pretend to be in the movement and are probably spies for the government. And so on another level, they don't see why I should be any different."

"And what do you think about that?"

"Well . . ." She paused again, as if studying something on the field, except this time there were no cheerleaders—just one skinny ninth grader running laps in shorts that were too short. "I agree that what my father is trying to do is more important than anything in my life could be. But still . . ."

She looked at me, as if wanting me to finish the sentence for her. I nodded, hoping she would understand that I got what she meant.

"Trade you for half your sandwich," she offered, handing me the container of rice with cold vegetables she brought every day.

"Really?"

I love every kind of Asian food, as I had told her. She said she would take bread over rice anytime.

"So what got you interested in China?" she asked after we had swapped lunches. "I mean, I know you take great satisfaction in knowing more than Mr. Stoltz does, but there has to be more to it than that."

Besides, that's a pretty low bar, I thought. But I didn't say it.

"Well, that *is* good motivation," I said. "But—" I paused, and then thought, What the heck. What's the worst that can happen?

So I took a deep breath, screwed up my courage—feel free to add any cliché that comes to mind—and said, "It's kind of a long story. Maybe we could do something Saturday? Go to the Freer or something?"

I went back to my rice as if it were no big deal whether she said yes or no, and thought, Did you really just ask yourself what's the worst that can happen? How about she turns you down? Or laughs?

Or even worse, politely blows you off in a way you know is designed not to hurt your feelings?

"The Freer?" Ti-Anna repeated.

"The gallery?" I said. "On the Mall?"

I started chattering nervously. "There's an exhibit of ancient jades and bronzes that's supposed to be pretty cool. Late Shang dynasty, early Western Zhou . . ."

"Okay, now you're just showing off," Ti-Anna said. "*Nobody's* heard of the Shang dynasty. I'm not even sure there *was* a Shang dynasty."

Around 1600 B.C.E. to 1060 B.C.E., if you want to know. Not as important as the Qing or Ming dynasties, it's true, but it had its moments.

But I let that pass.

"It sounds fun," Ti-Anna said as though she meant it. "Let's see how much homework we end up with, and if it's not too bad I'll ask my mother."

Knowing how seriously Ti-Anna took her homework, and having seen how eager her mother was for Ti-Anna to know me, I wasn't encouraged.

But I also didn't think Ti-Anna was the kind to say things just to be polite.

Sure enough, late Friday afternoon she called and asked what time we should meet. We agreed on noon at the Bethesda Metro station.

"By the way, Janice wants to come too," she said. "Is that okay?"

What could I say?

Chapter 6

We had to wait for a train, like you do sometimes on weekends, so we stood around making awkward chitchat on the platform.

When we finally boarded, the car was mostly empty. The girls sat on a two-person bench, and I sat across the aisle. They gossiped. I pretended to use my phone. (I don't get service on the Metro.) The expedition was beginning to feel like a big mistake.

But as the train slowed into Dupont Circle, they both stood up. Janice gave Ti-Anna a quick hug, shot me a breezy "Bye, Ethan" and jumped off. Ti-Anna nudged my shoulder. "Slide over," she said.

"Did I say something wrong?" I asked.

"Oh, it has nothing to do with you," Ti-Anna answered. "Janice wouldn't be caught dead in a museum."

"So why did she come?"

"Well, my mother suggested I ask her," Ti-Anna said. "So I did. She'll take the bus over to Georgetown and meet some other friends and have a fine afternoon shopping."

I guess I looked surprised. Ti-Anna looked at me and then looked away.

"I'm usually totally honest with my mother," she said. "But I thought, how ridiculous is it to worry about my going to the Freer Gallery with someone as, well, wholesome as Ethan Wynkoop?"

"Thanks a lot," I said. She laughed. At least she hadn't said "harmless." Or "dorky."

We rode the rest of the way in what I thought was a comfortable silence. And when we got to the Freer, we did amble through the exhibit. We did both notice a figurine of a small toad that looked a lot like Mr. Stoltz.

But I'm afraid I can't tell you much more about the ancient jades and bronzes of the Shang dynasty, or the Western Zhou, for that matter. We were so focused on our conversation that we (or at least I) didn't notice much else.

At one point I asked about her friendship with Janice. "You seem so, well—"

"Different from each other?"

I nodded.

"I think that's one reason we've always gotten along so well," Ti-Anna said. "She's not dumb, but she likes having fun. Music, clothes, the usual. She jokes that all she wants to know about China is how to pick out a pattern when she gets married. If you knew my parents, you'd get why that's appealing."

"They never do anything fun?"

"Not often."

On hot summer Sundays, she said, her father loved to rent a rowboat at Seneca State Park and take the family out on the lake.

"He goes in his long pants and black shoes, and spreads a handkerchief over his bald spot, and looks totally ridiculous, but he doesn't care," she said. "He's very proud of his skill as a rower."

Once, she said, a thick black snake wriggled under their boat, and Ti-Anna's mother was so startled she flung her straw hat into the water. Her father started to laugh, and when neither Ti-Anna nor her mother dared put her hand in to retrieve the hat, he laughed harder, and pretty soon they all had tears rolling down their cheeks. Ti-Anna laughed just thinking about it.

"But there aren't too many times like that," I suggested.

She shook her head.

"What about you?" she asked. "You promised to explain how you got interested in all this." By now we were sitting on a bench in the Freer's shady courtyard.

I told her how when I was a kid I'd gotten interested in hieroglyphics and the methods archaeologists had used to puzzle out their meaning. Which had led me to Chinese characters, so different from our puny twenty-six letters. Which led, somehow, to Asian martial arts.

"But of course I couldn't go to the karate place in Bethesda like everyone else," I said. "Somehow I fixed on a kendo studio across the county."

"Kendo?"

"Japanese swordsmanship," I said. "I still train there a couple of times a week."

I tried to explain why I liked it so much—the predictability, the ritual, how bit by bit and with a lot of hard work you can feel yourself getting quicker and more balanced, but how when you reach a higher level you always discover something you didn't know or couldn't do.

The master at the studio had taken me and my friend James under his wing, taught us to use chopsticks at the Korean restaurant down the block, lent us books on Japan and Korea (where James's parents came from) and then, when I had devoured those, on China.

"For some reason, I fell in love with China," I said.

The Great Wall. The Mongol hordes. The court rituals, the sages, the emperors who had hundreds of their concubines buried alive with them when they died—I soaked it all in. China's civilization is four thousand years old. Comparing China to America is like putting a hundred-year-old guy next to a kindergartner. The Chinese invented not just gunpowder and rockets and fireworks, which everyone knows about, but earthquake detectors, printing presses, even toilet paper. And their art is amazing.

"Then I started reading about modern China," I said. I began with Edgar Snow's book about Mao and the Long March, with its romantic view of the Communists, the hardships they endured before taking power, the poverty of the peasants they wanted to help. Then I started reading memoirs of the Cultural Revolution and realized things were a bit more complicated.

"So who's James?" Ti-Anna asked after I had finished rattling on. We had left the museum and were walking slowly up Fourteenth Street, toward the White House.

"I met him at kendo, and even though he lived pretty far away we became best friends," I said. "Our parents got us each an Xbox so we could play together without them having to drive one of us to the other's house all the time."

"What happened to him?"

"He moved with his family to New York a couple of years ago," I said. "I visited him the first summer, but it wasn't the same."

I might have explained how empty it felt to visit a best friend who for no good reason wasn't a best friend anymore. But we had reached the Metro station. And by the time we boarded a train, Ti-Anna seemed to have lost interest, almost as if I'd said something wrong.

I realized soon enough that I'd been right about something distracting her. But it wasn't anything I'd said.

Chapter 7

It was almost two weeks later that she confided in me.

Things had been going well between us. In fact, my main worry was how I'd manage to keep seeing her during the summer.

And then, at lunch, on a Thursday, she sat down and said, "My father is gone."

Actually, she sat down and didn't say anything for a long time.

She hadn't brought lunch. She waved away my sandwich.

I asked what was wrong, and that only made her look more as though she would cry.

Then, finally, she told me.

"What do you mean, gone?" I asked.

I knew her father traveled sometimes—to conferences in Providence, or Vancouver, or Berkeley. He could hardly afford it, but activists in a town would raise enough money to pay his expenses and a bit more, to hear him speak. Sometimes Ti-Anna would go along, helping translate, but often he went on his own. So his being away was nothing unusual.

"He's disappeared," Ti-Anna said, almost without expression.

She looked around as if someone might be eavesdropping, but of course there was no one. It was a normal sunny day on the track-and-field bleachers.

I waited for her to explain, and gradually she did, in bits and pieces.

Two weeks earlier, she said, her father had flown, much to her mother's dismay, to Hong Kong.

This was news to me.

"I know, I know," she said. "I didn't tell you. My dad is totally paranoid about the agents keeping tabs on him, and it's just easier if I can answer honestly when he asks, 'You haven't mentioned this to anyone, right?' And it didn't seem like such a big deal."

I nodded. I believed it wasn't that she didn't trust me.

"So what was he doing? I thought he wasn't allowed to go back to China?"

"He's not," Ti-Anna answered. "But he thought Hong Kong might be different."

Hong Kong, I knew, is a gray zone, part of China but with its own government and more freedom. It was a British colony for a hundred years, and when Britain gave it back in 1996, China promised not to impose its Communist system. So far they've kept the promise.

"Even so, he wasn't sure if they'd let him in once he landed."

"So why did he go?"

She shook her head. "I'm not sure. He's always looking to get in touch with people on the inside. Like I told you, he believes China is just a spark away from a democratic revolution, and nothing will ever stop him from thinking so. He must have gotten some news from someone he trusted that a meeting could be arranged or something like that."

"Your mother has no clue?"

She shook her head again. "She's practically catatonic."

26

Her dad had called once to report that the immigration people in Hong Kong had let him in. Ti-Anna and her mother didn't know where he was staying, but he'd bought a SIM card and told them he'd call to let them know he was all right.

He had called once more. And then nothing. Radio silence. Not a word.

"Maybe he's really busy," I suggested. "Maybe his phone died and he forgot his charger."

Ti-Anna gave me one of her little half smiles. "My father doesn't leave things like that to chance," she said.

Then she did start to cry, big, almost silent sobs that shook her narrow body. "Something is wrong. Something has happened."

I wanted to put my arm around her hunched shoulders, but I didn't. After a minute the sobs stopped. She wiped her cheeks with the back of her hand.

"We called the Hong Kong trade office here, and they claim not to know anything—said they didn't even have a record of his landing, which is odd, since we know he landed."

She'd emailed her father, even though before he left he'd told them not to, and gotten no reply. The people at the embassy despised him, there was no point in calling them, but Ti-Anna had called her father's friend on the China desk of our State Department. He had made inquiries, and the Chinese claimed to have no information.

"My mother is paralyzed with fear," she said. "She was furious at me for making any calls. She thinks if we call any friends in Hong Kong we'll get them in trouble and make things worse for my dad."

She sighed. "Short of going to Hong Kong, I don't know what else to do," she said.

I'd say that was the moment when the trouble started.

Chapter 8

I could complain about my dad: how he isn't around enough, how he drifts off in the middle of a conversation when he's focused on a physics problem. But really, he is a good father. If I lost him, I would never be the same. Ever. I know that. And to not even be able to say good-bye . . .

What must she be feeling?

After school the next day I biked to the Barnes & Noble, bought the densest, smallest-type guidebook to Hong Kong I could find and biked home.

I liked to think of myself as someone who cared about people's rights. I'd stay up reading about a Burmese monk who had walked straight at soldiers with their guns pointed at him, the monk carrying nothing but a begging bowl and his belief in freedom, because— because why? I couldn't quite fathom it. Because it was the right thing to do.

I'd think, Would I have the guts? Would I ever do *anything*? Or would I just read? And mouth off in history class?

In ninth grade I'd started a human rights club. The idea was to pick a prisoner of conscience somewhere and start a letter-writing campaign.

Only a few people showed up for the first meeting, and fewer for the next. I never called a third. I blamed the other kids, but it was my fault. I didn't like clubs. I didn't want to share my obsessions with people I hardly knew.

Here was a chance to do something.

If I could just get to Hong Kong, Ti-Anna had said. Well, why not? Wasn't her father's cause more important than anything in our piddly tenth-grade lives?

I sat at my desk, my world history textbook propped up in front of me. Our final was in two days. I wasn't taking in a word.

Ti-Anna had looked so miserable. And so alone. I was the one person she trusted. Would it be so crazy to try to help a friend?

If she were in Hong Kong, Ti-Anna had told me, she could track her father's movements. People who were afraid to talk over the phone would be more open face to face.

I slammed the textbook shut and went downstairs. My parents weren't home. At the back of my mom's closet, behind the shoes, with the other important documents—like her favorite drawings of mine from elementary school—I found my passport.

We'd gone to the post office to apply for it two years earlier, when my parents had announced that we were going to take a family vacation to Mexico. We never take family vacations, and sure enough, at the last minute one of them was nearing some breakthrough and we didn't go. But the passport had arrived and was valid for another three years.

"Honestly, I don't think he's dead," Ti-Anna had said.

I had winced, but she hadn't.

"Because if he were, why wouldn't the Hong Kong police tell us? Even if *they*"—and here she hadn't meant the Hong Kong police—"had killed him, they would want to cover up *how* he had died, not *that* he had died."

I gave up pretending to study, lay down on my bed, read the guidebook from preface to index and then started at the beginning again.

Ti-Anna had tried to persuade her mother that the two of them should fly over, but her mother wouldn't budge. It wasn't so much the money, she had told me, though that was scary enough. The real problem was that her mother was used to following instructions. Living in a strange country, she'd never learned much English. She hardly ventured beyond the bus route between their apartment and the grocery store. When there was a problem with a bill, Ti-Anna would handle it.

Ti-Anna's mother was pulling even further into her shell with her husband having disappeared. She was sure he would call, or so she said, and she didn't want to be away from the phone even for a second until he did. Ti-Anna was grocery shopping for the two of them.

I went online and studied airline schedules and visa rules and currency exchange rates. We can do this, I thought.

Why not? I asked myself.

Because it is crazy, I answered. You *know* it's crazy.

I decided that at lunch on Monday, after our world history exam, I'd tell Ti-Anna what I had figured out.

Chapter 9

We had agreed to meet out on the bleachers, in our usual spot, with whoever finished first waiting for the other. It was me; I couldn't stand to go back and review my answers once I finished a test, whereas Ti-Anna liked to use as much time as they gave you.

So I waited.

"It's so hot," she said when she finally came out and sat down. She stood right up again. I followed her back toward school and around to the front, where a giant old oak shaded the lawn.

We didn't talk about the exam. It wasn't that long ago that I had dreamed about how happy I'd be when tenth grade was over. Now it didn't matter.

I had made two sandwiches, figuring her mother wasn't doing much cooking, and I handed her one. She stared at it like she wasn't sure what she had in her hands or how it had gotten there.

I asked whether she had a passport.

"Of course," she said. Her father had wanted them to be ready to go back to China on a moment's notice, to jump when—as he was sure would happen—its frozen politics began to thaw.

"Good," I said. "I was thinking we could go to Hong Kong. You know. Together."

"What are you talking about?" Ti-Anna asked.

Speaking in a rush so she couldn't break in, I explained my plan. I told her that you didn't need a visa to go to Hong Kong. I'd scoped out the cheapest tickets. We could charge them, go for a week, find her dad and get home before the charges showed up on my mom's account. By then, if we'd succeeded, how could anyone object?

It took her a few seconds to process what I was saying

"Ethan, why would your parents pay for me to go to Hong Kong?" she said. "And why would they let you go to Hong Kong for something that has nothing to do with you?"

I have to admit, that stung.

Which maybe showed on my face, because in a softer voice she said, "Listen, I appreciate what you're offering, really I do. But how could I let you pay for me to go to Hong Kong? Or go with me? It could be really dangerous."

"I've thought all that through," I said. "Your father, and what he stands for, are more important than either of us, right? You've said so yourself. I wouldn't be paying for you, but for democracy in China. And you could pay me back, eventually. Well, my parents. You'd pay them back.

"And as for danger," I continued bravely, "I think you'd be in less danger if I were with you."

She gave me one of her looks. "Because your Chinese is so fluent? Or is it your kung fu skills you have in mind?"

"Ha ha," I said. "Kendo, not kung fu. What I have in mind is that I'm an American-born, middle-class kid from a nice middle-class suburb, no connection to anything political—*they* would know that if I disappeared, there would be a pretty big fuss, don't you think?"

I tried to say *they* with the right intonation, as if I'd been keeping an eye on Chinese security goons all my life.

For the first time Ti-Anna seemed to think seriously about my idea.

"Ethan, you think your parents will say 'Sure, go ahead, take a trip to the other side of the world with some girl we've never met to find her missing father'?"

"Ah, well," I said. "That is a good question. So we come up with a better idea: ask permission, but only after we get back."

As it happened, my parents were both at their annual conference in Geneva. When I was little, they used to take turns going, my mom one year, my dad the next. Now they felt comfortable leaving me on my own.

My big brother, who lived not far away in College Park, was supposed to look in on me. (My sister lives in Pittsburgh.) But he was almost as absentminded as our parents, and not all that wild about babysitting. So I thought I could persuade him that I'd gone to New York to visit James, like I had a couple of summers before, and that he'd known about the trip all along but hadn't been paying attention when my mother explained it to him. It wouldn't be the first time.

"Not an option for me," Ti-Anna said. "Not with my mother."

"No," I said. "I see that. We'd have to figure that one out."

Lost in thought, chewing on the sandwich without seeming to notice, let alone appreciate, that I'd added jam to the peanut butter, Ti-Anna didn't answer for a long time.

Then she looked at me with a half smile, as if to say, maybe it's not such a crazy idea after all.

Of course, we had no idea right then how crazy an idea it was. By the time we did realize, it was way too late.

Chapter 10

Through the rest of exam week I tried to study as if everything were normal while also booking flights, changing money, poring over maps. Two worlds, one purpose: to keep from thinking about what I was about to do.

Because when I did think about it, I was terrified. Ironically, the calmer and more convinced Ti-Anna became, the more terrified I felt, and the guiltier about some of the things we were about to do.

I had learned that the airline required minors traveling alone to have a signed letter from their parents. And even though we would have letters by the time we got on the Metro to go downtown and find the Metrobus that would take us to Dulles airport, it wasn't our parents who would have signed them.

Then there was the email I sent my brother just before shouldering my backpack—well, actually, *his* backpack, but I didn't think he'd need it in the next week.

Think I can make the ten a.m. Vamoose bus, I wrote. See you in a few days. I watered the plants.

The Vamoose goes from Bethesda to Penn Station in New York

City. I emailed instead of texting, because my brother doesn't check his email that often. I said that I *could* make the ten a.m. bus; I didn't say I was *going* to. And I had in fact watered the plants.

When I thought about what I was doing, I knew I shouldn't excuse myself, because I *was* trying to give my brother the wrong idea, and I knew my parents would never approve. Instead, I justified my actions by telling myself I was going to explain everything as soon as we got back. If I was being dishonest, it was only for a short time.

Ti-Anna said she would never disrespect her mother that way, even if it were possible. She'd decided to explain everything in a letter, leave it on the kitchen counter and slip out early, before her mother woke up. Well, not everything: she didn't mention me.

She knew how upset her mother would be. But she promised to be careful, and she promised to be in touch soon, and there was plenty of food in the apartment. She told herself her mother would be all right, and she was pretty sure her mom wouldn't do anything to stop us. Whom would she call, after all?

And once we found Ti-Anna's dad, all would be forgiven.

Chapter 11

As we rode the escalator down to the Metro, though, it really began to sink in.

Not that long ago Ti-Anna had been riding these same stairs a step below me, like now, laughing with Janice and pretending not to notice how sulky I was that Janice had come along and how nervous I was about our first sort-of date.

Now I stared at Ti-Anna's tight ponytail. Her neck and shoulders were taut, her body tense with the misery of deserting her mother. And I thought: This time you *should* be nervous.

It sank in a little deeper when, as we boarded the subway, I noticed a man boarding the same car through a different door. Navy suit, hair cut short on the sides and standing up on top, an alert way of taking everything in while seeming not to look at anything. A man, in other words, a lot like the ones I'd seen in the blue Taurus across from Ti-Anna's apartment.

When he stood as we stood, as the train approached Farragut North, I thought: It's not too late to forget the whole thing.

But he wasn't on the escalator as we left the station. I didn't see him following us to the bus stop, or in line with us there, or on the airport bus after we found seats toward the back. I told myself to stop being paranoid and relax.

And though I wouldn't say I relaxed, for a while everything did go more smoothly than I had expected. Ti-Anna and I had worked out our stories, in case anyone asked: she was visiting relatives; I was going to stay with her while I worked on a summer service project.

But no one asked. The check-in lady never asked for our letters, maybe because she was so harried by all the families with mounds of luggage and crying babies and kids hooking and unhooking the line dividers.

Check-in, security, X-ray—it all went smoothly, like this was something we did every month. I thought my phone might not work from Hong Kong, so from the boarding area I sent one last message to my brother: Made it. Everything fine. Once again, not technically a lie.

And then we were on the jumbo jet, squished into middle seats way at the back. The plane taxied, took off, leveled. Ti-Anna turned on her iPod and closed her eyes. Now, I thought, you can relax.

Instead, it *really* hit me. What on earth were we doing? What had I been thinking? New York City was the most exotic place I'd ever been. Now, just because I had read about China, I thought I could make my way in a huge strange city, with nobody knowing where I was, and no idea where to go? What had I been *thinking*?

Then I glanced over at Ti-Anna. She had pushed her seat back a few inches, and her eyes were closed, so I could really look—the dark eyebrows, the cheekbones. That vulnerable hollow at the base of her neck. Her serious mouth, which could take you by such surprise with one of her unexpected smiles.

A smile I'd hardly seen since her father had disappeared. Luckily, right about then, they came around with food. Ti-Anna took out her earbuds and we studied the movie listings as we ate, and I began to feel better. When I asked the attendant, simply as a point of useful information, how long it would be until the next meal, she brought me a second dessert, at which point Ti-Anna plugged back into her iPod and pretended not to know me.

A few minutes later, though, I noticed a half smile on her face, so I tapped her hand and asked what she was listening to.

She slipped off her earbuds and said, "The only thing I've ever seen my parents dance to."

They'd been invited to Janice's bat mitzvah, she said. About an hour into the party, her mother took her dad's hands, pulled him up and led him to the dance floor.

"It was Taio Cruz," Ti-Anna recalled. "But they were dancing cheek to cheek, like it was Frank Sinatra or something."

"Sounds mortifying."

"At first," she said. "But they both looked so happy. I thought— it's hard to explain—I thought, this is who they might have been, if their world had been different."

"Or if he hadn't decided he needed to change that world," I said.

The attendants dimmed the lights and told people in the window seats to pull down the shades. Everyone around us was dozing. Ti-Anna asked if I remembered the first time I'd heard of her father.

"When I was reading about the Democracy Wall," I said. "I thought that was so amazing."

In 1979, when China was just recovering from the Cultural Revolution, a few people started painting big character posters and hanging them on a park fence in Beijing. The posters talked about how modernization couldn't be only about getting rich but had to lead to liberty too. For a while the reform wing of the Party let it go on, but eventually they got nervous and shut it down.

"That's when I got interested in your dad and people like him," I said. He'd been a student back then. "People who will risk everything for what they know is right."

41

You could find them, I had discovered, anywhere governments tried to keep people from saying what they want to say—Venezuela, Ethiopia, Russia. They would write letters, give speeches, organize protests, knowing they would get thrown in jail, beaten up, tortured, maybe put in solitary confinement and forgotten.

But the Democracy Wall—there was something completely Chinese about it too: China had always had its Confucian scholars and poets willing to speak truth to power.

"It takes an incredible certainty about what's right and what's wrong, I guess," I said.

Ti-Anna nodded. "Probably it's a good thing that only a few of us are born with that," she said.

While I was mulling that over, she put her earbuds back in and closed her eyes.

When I thought I glimpsed the guy in the blue suit sitting a ways ahead of us, I didn't say anything. If I was having paranoid fantasies, there was no point in alarming Ti-Anna too. And if she thought I was so nervous that I was already having paranoid fantasies, she'd regret coming with me before we even landed.

Which we did (land, that is), about fourteen hours after we'd taken off. And which it seemed she did (regret, that is), pretty much as soon as we were on the ground.

But Ti-Anna's moods could go up and down. That was one of the many things I would learn over the next nine days.

Day One: Sunday

Hong Kong

Chapter 12

I don't know if I can make you understand how spectacular Hong Kong is, even if you've seen some of those cheesy movies that supposedly take place there. Especially if you've seen those movies—Hong Kong is nothing like that.

Imagine six million people living on a few tiny islands and a little fingernail of mainland China, crowding in more and more every year, and as they get more and more crowded, building in the only direction they have to go: up.

Escalators run up hills along sidewalks, and skyscrapers jostle each other as if they're stretching to escape each other's shadows. Even the buses and trolleys have two stories. And it's all so noisy and jumbled and packed in that for me it was exhausting just to think about living there.

The harbor is crazily alive, with ferries zigging and zagging past each other, and hundreds of people jockeying to spring off as soon as each ferry docks. A mountain soars up from the harbor—the center of Hong Kong Island—and beyond that, hundreds of smaller islands, some tiny, some with perfect little beaches, some so green and tropical-feeling you can't believe you're in one of the most crowded city-states in the world.

Of course, I didn't see all that at first. I was so worried about Ti-Anna's mood that I didn't notice much of anything.

It felt as though Ti-Anna had given up before we'd even started. She let me lead her through passport control and to the baggage carousel. She followed me through customs and out into the gleaming terminal, and just stood there while I tried to figure out the best way into the city.

The answer to that, by the way, is: subway. There's a beautiful new system, and it whisks you into town.

But if you want to know how *we* went, the answer is: bus. The bus was a lot cheaper, and I was worried that my credit card might not work at ATMs in Hong Kong, or that there'd be some limit on how much I could withdraw before it froze up or sent an emergency message. Then even my absentminded mother, deep into her Geneva conference, might wonder who was using her card in Hong Kong.

The day before we'd left Washington I'd gone downtown and changed some U.S. money for Hong Kong money—theirs are called dollars too, but one U.S. dollar gets you about six of theirs—so I had enough to get us started. But I still didn't want to spend more than we had to.

We took the A21 bus into town. When we alighted, I unfolded my map.

"According to the book, the cheapest places to stay are in one huge old building here," I said, pointing to the map. "We're here. I think we can walk."

"Okay." Ti-Anna shrugged, without so much as glancing down. She lifted her bag onto her shoulder and again just stood there, waiting for me to lead.

I didn't say anything. I reminded myself she was still feeling

46

terrible about the way she'd left her mom, and of course she was thinking about her father, too, and being in Hong Kong made that more scary. And it was morning in Hong Kong, and neither of us had slept much.

But still. I was beginning to wonder if she was letting me make all the decisions so that when things went wrong I would get all the blame. I couldn't help remembering how sure she'd sounded when she'd said she could track her father down if only she got to Hong Kong. She didn't look so confident now—and it wasn't like I'd have the first clue where to start.

Okay, don't get ahead of yourself, I thought. Sweat trickled down the small of my back. Even though it was Sunday, the street was so noisy you practically had to shout. I was so tired I thought I might fall asleep standing up.

Find a room with a couple of beds with nice clean sheets, I told myself. Take a cool shower. Everything will look better. Even to Ti-Anna.

Good advice. Except I wasn't sure we would ever get there.

Chapter 13

We found the building after a hot, crowded walk up Nathan Road. It was about as peculiar as anything I'd ever seen.

You had to walk down a long, shadowy passageway with stores on either side selling cameras and calculators and a lot of junk you couldn't imagine anyone would ever buy. Every now and then you'd pass a bank of elevators and a list of hotels, and you had to take an elevator to the one you'd chosen.

I figured the deeper in we went, the cheaper the hotels might get. We walked to the shaft labeled E and looked at the list.

"How about Rising Phoenix Guesthouse?" I said. "That sounds good."

Ti-Anna looked at me as though I was a hopeless case, but she seemed past caring. We stepped into an elevator like a coffin, with one grayish fluorescent bulb flickering.

The doors did not open onto the cheerful lobby I'd been picturing. Instead we had to walk so far down a dim corridor that I began to have trouble breathing. What would happen in a fire?

Eventually we came to a high desk on the left. The clerk behind it was young and fat and looked bored. He eyed us disdainfully.

I waited for a moment, thinking that maybe Ti-Anna would pitch in here with her Chinese. But no. Nothing.

So I tried in English, asking if there was a room available. The clerk looked us over for a minute, as if he hadn't heard a word, and then reached behind him without turning his head, grabbed a key attached to a big wooden knob and pushed it across the desk.

"Two hundred dollars," he said, and not as though it were the beginning of a negotiation.

I gasped, then remembered he was talking about Hong Kong dollars. I reached for the key. He snatched it away, a lot faster than you might expect for a guy his size, and said, "Pay first."

I counted out the colorful bills and reached for the key again, and again his big soft hand was quicker than mine. Obviously he enjoyed this little game.

"Passports," he said.

We handed them over. He glanced at the photos, then at each of us, without apparent interest, and slowly, deliberately entered something from each passport into his computer. I was swaying with fatigue.

Finally, he slid the passports and key across the desk.

"Fourth door on left," he said. "Showers last door on right. Fifty cents a shower. No music, no food, no smoking."

In the shower? I wanted to ask. But I picked up the passports and key—he didn't fight me for it this time—and we headed even deeper down the Corridor of Doom.

Nothing could be more depressing than this, I thought—until we found Room 23, managed in the gloom to work the key and banged open the door.

I fumbled for the switch, and a harsh overhead light flickered on. Two narrow beds filled the room. You could sidle between them, but there was no room to put a suitcase down. On each mattress were a couple of gray sheets and what was supposed to be a towel. A filthy window overlooked an air shaft. Splotches where people had flattened roaches and mosquitoes dotted the walls like acne.

I thought it might send Ti-Anna over the edge. She pushed in next to me, slung her duffel on a bed and unfolded a towel. It was about the size of a dinner napkin.

"Maybe it's a diaper for the Rising Phoenix," she said, and, to my astonishment, began to laugh. Her laughing got me laughing and, even though there was nothing very funny, in a minute we had fallen on the hard mattresses with tears rolling down our cheeks.

"So," I finally said. "Do you think these hotels are all like this?"

"You mean, or did we just get lucky?" Ti-Anna said. And we started laughing again.

"I call first shower," she said. The real Ti-Anna was back.

Chapter 14

I suppose you might be thinking that there could be worse things than sharing a hotel room with a beautiful girl in an exotic city a long, long way from your parents and (as far as we knew) from hers.

I suppose, if the situation had been different, I might have been thinking the same.

But I can promise you that if you'd been in *this* situation— scared, exhausted, overwhelmed by the foreignness of everything— romance would have been the last thing on your mind.

We each took a fifty-cent shower—I won't even *try* to describe the showers—and collapsed on our beds without bothering to spread out the sheets. It took somewhere between five and seven seconds to fall into a dead sleep.

When I awoke I had no idea where I was. Then I saw the splotches on the wall.

I swung my feet into the narrow space between our beds. Ti-Anna was in fresh clothes, her hair brushed, smiling. She must have shaken me awake. Out the air shaft, you couldn't tell whether it was morning, noon or night. Or winter or summer, for that matter.

"What time is it?" I asked groggily.

"Dinnertime," she said. "C'mon, let's go explore."

After I brushed my teeth in the yellowing little sink in the corner, we stepped out and I locked the door. Before I could head to the elevator, Ti-Anna whispered, "Hold on."

She yanked a strand of hair from her scalp and, kneeling, wound it around the door handle and then across to a nail that was poking out of the doorframe.

"What are—" I started, but she shook her head and shushed me.

The looming desk clerk stared suspiciously as we walked past him to the elevators. We waited again for forever, rode the coffin down and made our way back out to Nathan Road.

And somehow, everything felt different. We were rested, an evening breeze had cooled things off, the people around us weren't in such a hurry. Ti-Anna seemed like herself again. Hong Kong felt like a magical place.

We walked to the harbor. Huge neon signs made everything brighter than daytime. Across the water the skyscrapers were putting on a show—not merely lit up, but with colored patterns dancing up and down the buildings and then skittering toward us in the reflection in the water below.

"Is it a holiday?" I asked a girl leaning on the railing next to me.

She laughed. "No, it's just Hong Kong," she said. "It's like this every night."

I turned back to the harbor but noticed a minute later that the girl was still looking at us and giggling as her friend whispered in her ear.

"What's so funny?" I asked.

"My friend was saying that even though your friend is not from here, she and I look like each other," she said. "I said, no, your friend is prettier." And she giggled some more.

There was some resemblance. The girl wore her hair like

Ti-Anna's and had the same longish face with high cheekbones and full lips.

"How do you know she's not from here?" I challenged. At which both of them burst into laughter again.

The question apparently was so silly that the girl, who turned out to be called Wei, didn't deign to reply.

"Is it your first time?" she asked.

We chatted with her and her friend Mai as we watched the Star Ferries come and go. They were high school kids like us, just hanging out, and we traded complaints about exams and homework and boring teachers. It felt good to be having a conversation about normal things.

Eventually we said we were hungry, and they told us they knew a great-but-cheap noodle restaurant. We tore ourselves away from the light show and let them lead us through a maze of streets so narrow that motor scooters were the biggest vehicles that could get through.

We came to a kind of outdoor café with two long, high tables with kerosene lanterns at each end. All along them young people perched on stools, chattering and slurping from huge, steaming bowls.

The girls installed us and helped us figure out the menu. They said they had to be home soon and couldn't stay to eat, but they sat next to us and didn't seem to be in any hurry to leave. Wei especially was a talker, asking lots of questions about America and excited at every answer. (We lived in *Washington*? Had we ever met the *president*?) All her questions ended in bubbly squeaks. All her statements ended with exclamation marks.

Finally, when our food came, Wei said they really, really had to go. They slid off their stools and left—only to return two minutes later.

"Oh!" Wei said, beaming proudly as she saw us eating. "I just wanted to make sure you could use chopsticks! You look like you've been doing it all your lives!"

This time, before leaving, she gave Ti-Anna her phone number and said to be sure to call if we had any trouble while we were in Hong Kong. And they were gone again, this time for good.

You can't imagine our trouble, I thought. But still. We'd made a couple of new friends.

Ti-Anna as usual didn't seem particularly hungry, but suddenly I was starving. Noodles with roasted pork had never tasted so good.

Only when we'd paid and were trying to find our way back through the maze to Nathan Road did I ask Ti-Anna about our hotel room door.

"A good-luck charm to keep the room safe?" I guessed.

"Not exactly," she said. "Listen, I'll be surprised if *they* don't try to track us, maybe bug our hotel room." It was that familiar "they" again. "The only question is how soon—if they've gone in already, we'll have some idea of what we're up against."

I felt like maybe I'd been reading too much nonfiction. I should have picked up a few more spy novels. "Where did you learn to do that?"

"It's not like my father and I didn't talk about stuff," she said.

"So if the hair is broken when we get back, it'll be bad news."

She nodded.

"And then?"

"Well," she said, "I have an idea."

She prodded me into something resembling a hardware store. The aisles were narrow and so crowded with junk that I could only follow her as she poked around. Eventually she settled on a couple of little knapsacks—the kind you might use if you were biking out to do a few errands—and air mattresses that folded down to almost nothing. I paid for them both.

Back on the street, she laid out what she had in mind. It sounded crazy, but I didn't have a better idea. And when we got to the room, she knelt in front of our door and soundlessly showed me two strands of hair, one hanging from the nail, the other from the doorknob.

She held her fingers to her lips—it wouldn't be safe to talk here anymore—and we went in to get some sleep.

The next day, we'd start looking for her father. And it seemed we might have company.

Day Two: Monday

Kowloon–Lamma Island–Hong Kong

Chapter 15

The mountainous desk clerk was still there in the morning when, following Ti-Anna's instructions, I approached to ask if we could keep the room for a week.

He swiveled to study his computer. Right, I thought, as if there's a long line for that particular cell. But I held my tongue.

"Twelve hundred dollars," he said.

That would give us a discount from the one-night rate, but not much of one, and Ti-Anna had told me to be sure to bargain. Easy for her to say: she was waiting in the room while the clerk glared at me. It was all I could do to keep from offering more than he'd asked for.

I counted out the bills. It about cleaned me out of Hong Kong money, but Ti-Anna had said, *Pay in advance: we want them to be sure we're staying put.* So I did.

We packed our knapsacks wordlessly, like we'd agreed the night before. Toothbrush, air mattress, a change of clothes, Hong Kong map. Passports, of course. When Ti-Anna wasn't looking, I slipped in my book, a biography of General MacArthur. The bags still looked small—as if we were heading out with guidebooks and cameras for a day of sightseeing.

We left everything else in the room, Ti-Anna's duffel neatly repacked, my stuff spilling onto the bed—a lived-in look, I thought.

As we headed back down the Corridor of Doom and into the coffin elevator, I hoped we would make it back at least once. I hated to think what my brother would say if I came home without his backpack. But I knew it might be a while. I can't say that I worried about missing the Rising Phoenix. I didn't think our clerk would miss us.

We walked down Nathan Road with throngs of commuters, all talking into their Bluetooths. At the first ATM, I decided we'd better find out if we could get money. I didn't like transmitting our location so soon, but it was that or go hungry. Going hungry is never a good option.

The screen was in Chinese, so I gave Ti-Anna the card and told her my password. We withdrew five hundred Hong Kong dollars and hoped we wouldn't set off alarms.

As we ferried across the harbor, the sun sparkled off the waves. Dozens of junks, patrol boats, barges and ferries crisscrossed before us and behind us. Off to the right you could see a navy destroyer, though I couldn't make out its flag.

We watched the ferrymen tie us to the dock and then stepped onto Hong Kong island. We were in Central, the heart of Hong Kong's financial district, at the height of rush hour, and people in dark suits were rushing all around us, toting briefcases and looking anxious. For a minute we stood close to each other, overwhelmed.

"Let's sit," Ti-Anna said.

We found a bench near someone selling boxes of juice and soy milk and cut-up pieces of pineapple from a cart. The pineapple looked juicy and sweet, but Ti-Anna, of course, didn't feel like eating.

"I know it's crazy, but I keep looking at faces," she said. "As if, if we sit here long enough, maybe he'll just appear out of the crowd."

"And spoil our fun?"

Ti-Anna smiled politely. We breathed in ocean smells and city fumes, listened to flags snapping and buses grinding their gears. People streamed past as if they all had someplace they had to be five minutes ago.

Our first stop, Ti-Anna had said the night before, would be Horace Kwan, one of her father's oldest friends. I'd heard of him. For years he had been a leader of Hong Kong's pro-democracy camp. While Hong Kong was a British colony, until 1996, he'd agitated for more self-rule. After Britain handed Hong Kong back to China, he'd kept on agitating for self-rule, only now his target was Beijing, not London.

"If my father was in Hong Kong, I'm sure he would have seen Horace," Ti-Anna had said.

If? I'd thought. I'd never heard her doubt that her dad at least had started here.

Horace Kwan didn't know we were coming, and we didn't know if he'd even be in his office. He'd been on the legislative council—like Hong Kong's Congress—but now he was semiretired from politics. He was still a lawyer, though, Ti-Anna had said, and a successful one. I figured the earlier we got there, the better the chance we'd find him before he went to court or somewhere else.

I took out the map once more, though I'd pored over it after dinner and was pretty sure which way to head. Ti-Anna quit examining the men passing before us. We walked past a couple of cool old buildings from colonial days and some great-looking palm trees—which I had never seen in real life—but mostly there were skyscrapers, each one sleeker and taller than the next.

Kwan's was one of the sleekest, all intimidating marble and glass. In the lobby two young women in powder-blue suits with powder-blue caps sat behind a desk, but they didn't seem to be blocking anyone from the bank of elevators. Trying to look like we knew what we were doing, we found Horace Kwan on the directory on the wall—floor 33—and joined the flow of people riding up.

Double glass doors led to a thickly carpeted anteroom, where another young lady sat primly behind a wooden desk. It was weirdly quiet.

Ti-Anna found her voice first.

"We'd like to see Mr. Kwan, please," she said in English. I realized I had yet to hear her speak Chinese since we'd landed.

"Do you have an appointment?" the lady said.

She didn't exactly sneer, but she looked like she would have sneered if she hadn't been trained not to. Obviously, she knew the answer to her question.

Ti-Anna shook her head.

"Would you please tell him that Ti-Anna Chen is here? We don't mind waiting."

"I'm afraid Mr. Kwan doesn't see anyone without an appointment," she said.

"I understand," Ti-Anna said.

"Would you like to make an appointment?" the woman asked icily. "Though Mr. Kwan is quite booked for the next several months."

You had to know Ti-Anna to tell when she was angry. I could sense that she wasn't going to be inviting this woman to lunch any time soon.

"Would you please tell him that Ti-Anna Chen is here?" Ti-Anna repeated in a pleasant voice. "I think he might like to know."

The woman sighed, started to speak, glared at Ti-Anna and apparently decided that we weren't going anywhere. Shaking her head, she disappeared through a door in the wood-paneled wall behind her desk.

The door reopened almost instantly for a tall, distinguished man in a suit, with horn-rimmed glasses and a shock of black hair falling over his forehead.

"Ti-Anna?" he said. "Is it really you?"

She nodded. "And this is my friend Ethan."

"Horace Kwan," he said. He gravely shook my hand, then put a hand on Ti-Anna's shoulder without speaking.

Finally, he gestured toward the door.

"Please come in," he said.

Take that, I wanted to tell Miss Snooty, but she was nowhere to be seen.

Chapter 16

Stepping into Horace Kwan's office, you felt you might fall right into the harbor. The wall facing us was glass. You could see the Kowloon ferry dock we'd left from an hour before, and if you squinted and shielded your eyes from the sun bouncing off the waves you could even make out the railing where we'd met Wei and Mai.

"Please," Horace Kwan said again. "Do take a seat."

He pointed us toward a couch facing the glass and sat in an armchair to the side. His desk was at the other end of the room, dark wood with graceful curving legs.

Nobody spoke.

Well, I'm certainly not going first, I thought. But neither of them seemed uncomfortable. Horace Kwan was studying Ti-Anna as though if he looked hard enough he could read what was on her mind—but in a nice enough way, and she waited patiently.

Finally, he broke the silence.

"I've heard so much about you, for so long, Ti-Anna," he said. "This is a great pleasure." You could tell he meant it.

"I've heard a great deal about you, Mr. Kwan," she said.

There was another pause, and then he asked, "What brings you to Hong Kong? Are you meeting your father?"

"Well," Ti-Anna said. "We hope so. But that is why we came to see you. We don't know where he is."

I was studying his face, but I didn't see any change of expression—maybe a tensing, a slight leaning forward in his chair.

"What do you mean?" he said. "Please explain."

You could imagine his using the same calm tone for someone who came in and announced, "I just beheaded my husband," or something along those lines.

So Ti-Anna explained—how her dad had gotten a message that excited him, how he'd left for Hong Kong, how he'd hardly been in touch since—and how unusual that all was.

"I am certain that if he came to Hong Kong he would want to see you," she concluded. "So I thought you might be able to help us."

It was her turn to sound calm, but I knew she wasn't feeling calm. If Horace Kwan couldn't help, I wasn't sure where we'd go next.

He put his long fingers together in a steeple, searched Ti-Anna's face again and then glanced over at me.

Following his gaze, Ti-Anna said, "I have no closer friend than Ethan."

I blushed, and thought I'd tuck that away to replay later. I realized—I don't know why it hadn't occurred to me before—that if not for me they would have been speaking in Chinese.

"Well, then Ethan is my friend also," Horace said. "I'm sure you know"—he was looking at me now—"that Ti-Anna's father is one of our bravest and most important patriots."

Now it was Ti-Anna's turn to blush.

"Though you would not know it from Chinese newspapers today, I'm sure he will go down as such in our history books. If," he added drily, "Chinese students are ever permitted to study their true history."

He turned to Ti-Anna. "You know, this may surprise you, but I've always thought the bravest thing your father did was to leave the country," he said.

"To leave? Why was that brave?"

"He could have endured whatever they dished out in prison. But he knew how hard it is in China to be the family of a patriot—of a dissident, as they are called. I think he worried how much more your mother could stand, with him in jail and plainclothes police camped on the landing outside your apartment door, listening in on every phone call, following her on every trip to the market."

Ti-Anna perched on the edge of the sofa, facing Horace, totally still. I didn't know if she had any memory of those police guards. Somehow I was sure that she had never heard her parents talk about any of this.

"So," Horace said, "he left. Very difficult for him. He knew few would understand the different kind of courage required. He worried especially about the opinion of those who mattered most to him—especially his daughter."

I thought I might get teary, so I could only imagine how Ti-Anna must be feeling.

"He knew the normal fate of the exile—forgotten, overlooked, belittled. Somehow, if our suffering diminishes, then supposedly so does our moral authority. It is a strange calculus." He gazed out at his stunning view.

"In any case," he resumed. "Your father was determined to fight against this fate. Not for the sake of his ego, you understand, but for China. Even from America, he never stopped fighting for democracy in our homeland. And so, yes, I did see him here, quite recently, on his latest mission in that quest.

"He stopped in the day he arrived," Horace said. "Like you, he did not feel it necessary to make an appointment."

He smiled, and as he walked to his desk said, "You all must assume my business is doing very poorly, since you are sure you can drop in and find me available." He leafed back a page on his desk calendar. "The fourth, it was."

"And?" Ti-Anna said, her voice quavering slightly for the first time. "Did he tell you why he was here?"

Horace hesitated. "You must be hungry," he said. "Why don't we continue our conversation over dim sum?"

Before Ti-Anna could politely lie to him that we had already eaten, I interjected, "Yes!" It came out as a bit of a squawk. I realized, embarrassed, that it was the first word I had spoken.

But Ti-Anna didn't overrule me, and I realized, even more embarrassed, that his wanting to go out had nothing to do with food. He wanted to talk where he knew *they* would not be listening.

As he held the office door for us, he and Ti-Anna started conversing in Chinese. The young woman at the front desk gave me the evil eye as we walked out. I smiled back. We rode the elevator down in silence.

Chapter 17

I tried to memorize our route as Horace led, so that we could find our way back without him, but I soon gave up. He took us along skywalks and up and down escalators; only once did we come down to a road and have to wait at a traffic light.

He loped easily on his long legs, his shock of black hair bouncing lightly over his forehead. Ti-Anna walked beside him, chatting quietly.

Every once in a while I glanced over my shoulder, but if someone was following us, I didn't have a chance in a million of spotting him. I had thought New York City was crowded, but it couldn't match Hong Kong.

There was no hiding the Taurus parked across from Ti-Anna's apartment in Bethesda, and that was how they wanted it—to be visible, to be intimidating. The man on the Metro—if he was one of them—stood out from the crowd enough to be noticeable. But here, everyone was Chinese. Almost everyone was in suits. Not a few had military-style haircuts. There was just no way to know.

But if they cared enough to break into our hotel room, I had to assume they might care enough to keep an eye on us now.

Horace must have had the same idea, judging by how he behaved at the restaurant.

Inside the front door a half-dozen employees, each wearing headsets, manned a desk as people jostled to get their names on a list for tables. When the boss saw Horace, she made room through the crowd, led us to a bank of elevators—it seemed to be a four-story restaurant, crazy as that sounds—and escorted us to the third floor.

A wave of noise, a cheerful, hungry roar, nearly knocked us over as the elevator door opened on a huge room full of round tables. Before us a thousand people, or so it sounded, were eating and waving chopsticks and talking and arguing and drinking tea, while young women in uniforms pushed carts through the din, unloading little dishes at one table, then weaving on to the next and unloading some more.

The manager led us to a corner that I guessed was Horace's regular spot. But Horace whispered into her ear, and she led us right back into the middle of everything and plopped us at a table there.

"This way you can enjoy the true Hong Kong experience," Horace said to me with a polite smile. Yes, I thought, and this way no microphone could possibly pick up our conversation.

It wasn't easy to talk above the roar, anyhow, and for a while we concentrated on the food, or at least I did. Horace poured tea into our little round cups, and he said yes to almost every server who pushed a cart past us, until our table was covered with dishes of shrimp dumplings and pork wrapped in tofu skin and other things I didn't recognize and couldn't possibly name, even after tasting them.

Ti-Anna nibbled, Horace popped an occasional morsel, his chopsticks like extensions of his long fingers. I . . . well, I may have eaten more than my share. I already had spent enough time with Ti-Anna to know I'd better take advantage, because who knew when my next meal might be. Besides, I thought, it was only polite, as a guest, to show enthusiasm.

Finally, when every kind of cart had been wheeled past us, Horace leaned toward us and, in as quiet a voice as could be heard, asked Ti-Anna to retell her story, from the beginning.

She described her father's decision to go to Hong Kong, and how he had just disappeared after the second phone call, and how we had decided to follow. She ended with the broken hair and our plan to break free of the listeners.

Horace nodded gravely. "It is worrisome," he said. "I was certainly surprised to see you and your friend."

As far as I was concerned, that didn't advance things much. Ti-Anna nodded and waited.

"As you know, your father always believed that the key to bringing democracy to China would be uniting intellectuals like himself with workers from the factories," he said. "Many people argued against him. The workers are too busy making money and worrying about feeding their relatives back in the village, they would say. But he would say, no, the workers also want to be free, it is just a question of overcoming their fear."

I was sure none of this was new to Ti-Anna. But she listened without impatience. I tried to follow her example.

"When he came to see me, he was very excited, because he said he had a chance to meet with leaders of an underground workers' movement," Horace went on. "He seemed to think this could be the beginning of something big."

"Meet where?" Ti-Anna asked. "Inside China?"

Horace shook his head. "He didn't explain, and I didn't ask," he said. "But he told me the contact had come through a man who— well, do you know this name?" He slid an expensive-looking pen from his breast pocket and, rather than saying the name aloud, wrote three Chinese characters on a paper napkin, which he then swiveled so Ti-Anna could read it. She shook her head.

"He moved from the mainland to Hong Kong about fifteen years ago, I believe," Horace said, "probably barely in time to avoid arrest."

He crumpled the napkin into a ball and shoved it into his jacket pocket.

"He started a radio program that attracted a huge audience inside China. Every illegal strike, every workers' protest—somehow he would find out about it, and report on it, and people all through China would listen. Of course, no Chinese newspapers would write about such things."

He sipped his tea.

"A few years ago, his radio station said they would not carry his program anymore," Horace continued. "A business decision, they said—no advertisers. I'm sure there was pressure from Beijing." He spat that out with disgust.

"He kept his program going on the Internet. He still seems to hear more about what's happening inside China than anyone else, I don't know how. And somehow he earns enough of a living to keep going. I'm not sure how he manages that, either."

"So my father was going to meet him?"

Horace nodded. "If anyone knows where your father was headed, it would be he. Your father told me they were getting together the day after he saw me."

Whatever food remained on the table was looking a bit gelatinous. Horace signaled for a waitress, who came over and counted our plates to figure out how much we owed. He pulled some bills from his pocket. I offered to help pay, but he waved me off.

As the waitress walked away, Ti-Anna said, "Do you know how we can find this man?"

"He lives on Lamma—you know the island?"

74

Ti-Anna shook her head, but I said yes. I hadn't read and reread the guidebook for nothing. Lamma was just south of Hong Kong Island, and in a way its opposite—only a few thousand residents, in a few fishing villages. People from the city took the ferry there to go to the beach or eat seafood at restaurants on the bay.

"Do you know his number?" I asked.

"He has no phone, as far as I know," he said. "But I can give you an email address."

Ti-Anna shook her head. "Can you give us any more information? We need to pay him a visit."

"You and your friend are not exempt from dangers," Horace replied. "You cannot just roam about."

When Ti-Anna did not answer, he began drawing on another napkin.

"He lives on the most isolated part of the island—down here," he said as he sketched what looked like a long, narrow piece of a jigsaw puzzle. "The opposite end from where the ferry drops you."

This time I took the napkin, folded it and stuck it in my little pack.

"There are no cars on the island, as you know," he said to me. "If you don't have a boat, you have to walk. But once you get to his little bay, there's no missing the house and its bright red roof."

We headed for the elevator. He and Ti-Anna resumed talking in Chinese, this time very earnestly. As we rode down, I saw tears in her eyes. But by the time he shook our hands outside the restaurant and we again thanked him and said good-bye, she seemed calm.

"What was that about?" I asked.

"I asked if he would contact my mother," Ti-Anna said. "She will feel more reassured hearing from him."

"And what did he say?"

"He said we would be better off not pursuing this on our own, but that he would not try to stop us, since we had come so far and were so determined. He said my father would be proud of us. And he said he would tell my mother that I am fine, since it is true so far."

"Wow," I said. "'So far.' What does he think could happen?"

Ti-Anna shrugged. "He didn't strike me as full of optimism," she said. "But at least he didn't try to stop us."

Chapter 18

At first, things went according to Ti-Anna's plan, and I started to shake the ominous feeling Horace had left me with. Maybe I'd just eaten too many dumplings, I told myself.

We found our way back to the ferry docks. To be honest, I found our way; Ti-Anna's sense of direction was on a par with her appreciation for food.

We scoped out the piers, trying not to telegraph our interest in one over another. Ferries for Lamma seemed to depart every thirty minutes, from Pier 4.

At a kiosk, we bought a map of the island. Ti-Anna didn't want to leave such a clue, even with a harried clerk inside a kiosk, but I didn't think Horace's napkin would be enough to get us to Radio Man's house before dark. As a compromise we bought maps of a few other islands too.

I also insisted on buying some protein bars and Snickers, and a couple of Cadbury's Fruit and Nut bars—they still seemed to like their British sweets in Hong Kong.

"How can you even think about food after all that dim sum?" Ti-Anna said.

"You'll thank me later," I replied, thinking of it more as a suggestion than a prediction.

Joining the crowds in front of the main Star Ferry dock, we found places on a bench, sipping boxes of cold tea with our faces turned to the sun. The day was warming, though a cool breeze was blowing in from the bay. We could have been a couple of young tourists getting a lazy start on our sightseeing.

Sixty seconds before our ferry was supposed to leave, we tossed our tea boxes into the trash and moved fast, while trying to look like we weren't moving fast, toward the Lamma pier.

We stepped aboard just before one crewman shut the gate, while another tossed the lines from the giant knobs along the deck. We were the last ones on. If anyone wanted to follow us to Lamma, they'd have to take the next boat.

We made our way to the upper deck, found seats together on a bench, tucked our little packs between our feet and let our heart rates return to normal as the downtown receded and water sounds filled in where city sounds had been.

Oil tankers and cargo ships with giant containers stacked on their decks steamed smoothly past us, while fragile little fishing boats bounced in their wake. The warship I had noticed turned out to be from New Zealand. As we rounded the corner at the top of the island, the buildings gave way to woods, and the chop of the harbor gave way to bigger waves.

It was too windy to unfold the map, so we invented stories for the other passengers on the ferry. Those two boys with bicycles? Training for the Tour de France, but their parents didn't approve of them doing anything but studying, so they had to sneak over to Lamma to ride.

That plump young lady? Her pet turtle, which she loved more

than anything in the world, had died, and she was hoping to find a replacement in the wilds of Lamma, which was famous for its turtles.

As the island came into view, and the blur of green resolved into scrubby vines and banana trees, Ti-Anna grew serious again.

"He said one other thing to me on our way out of the restaurant," she said.

"Horace?"

She nodded. "On the way out, he said, 'Be careful about this man.'"

"Meaning Radio Man."

She nodded.

"What does that mean?"

She shrugged. "I don't know. But it doesn't really matter. Because if we don't get something from him, I don't know what we'll do."

So there was no Plan B? For a second, that made me mad. What if Kwan had been away when we got here? I had thought Ti-Anna knew a lot more than she was turning out to know.

Then I thought, if she's been fooling anyone, it's herself, not me. She wanted to think she had more to go on than she did, because she was that desperate.

And I thought, well, of course she's desperate. You would be too. Just because she always seems cool and controlled doesn't mean she has all the answers.

"Then we'll have to make sure we do get something from him," I said.

We picked up our backpacks and prepared to disembark. In an announcer's voice, I said, "Now approaching the strange and exotic island of Lamma. Please enjoy your stay, and do not cuddle the turtles."

Ti-Anna laughed, or tried to. We let the boys with bikes wheel off ahead of us, and then we jumped ashore.

Chapter 19

We set off immediately in the wrong direction. If anyone was going to report on our movements later, better that they see us leave the village the wrong way.

And it was a village—a few blocks, really, a street that curved along a not-too-appealing beach, lined with not-too-appealing restaurants. I supposed it would be festive at night, with terraces full of merrymakers and red lanterns bobbing in the breeze. But now, nearly deserted, with the sun spotlighting the mold-streaked walls and tin roofs, it all looked surprisingly old—as if it hadn't changed in fifty years. It was hard to believe we were only a few miles from the technoglass wonders of Hong Kong.

We headed north, away from the restaurants. For a while it seemed very tame, with every tree numbered, and a couple of golf cart–like things parked off to the side. The path was smoothly paved. We might have been in a theme park that had been abandoned a few years before. We even saw a turtle sunning on a rock right off the path—as if the Hong Kong Tourist Board had put it there for us.

But as we rounded the corner and left the village behind, the path started to get wilder. In half a mile or so, I saw what I'd been looking for: a dirt trail that doubled back behind the village, off the beaten track and toward the center of the island.

We started climbing. When we were well out of view of anyone on the paved path, I opened our map. The route looked like a straight shot—well, a winding shot, but only three miles or so to the other end of the island—and I thought we should be able to make it before nightfall, no sweat.

Ti-Anna waited patiently while I turned the map this way and that. She seemed to assume that if we started walking we would automatically end up at the right house, and map-reading was another one of my odd habits, like reading biographies of famous people. But she was willing to put up with it in a good-natured way.

The path was steeper and rougher than I had expected. The air was cooler than in the city, but I worked up a sweat as we climbed. The woods on either side of the path weren't high, but they were dense, with thick vines winding around each other and sometimes across the path. Atop one hill we came across a small Buddhist temple, red columns holding up a green-tiled, ski-jump roof, but it was untended, its paint peeling in the sea air.

We saw no one, though a couple of times I thought I heard someone, and we'd stop and hold still. Every now and then we'd break through to a view of a curving bay or beach way below us, on one side of the narrow island or the other. We saw no sunbathers. I supposed on a weekend there would be hordes.

At one point we stumbled on an abandoned house so decrepit that it could have been an ancient ruin, but for a rusty fan dangling from the ceiling and a lidless rice cooker forgotten in a corner. We sat on the cool cement floor for a few minutes and shared a protein bar.

"I think we're almost there," I said.

Ti-Anna didn't reply. I guessed she was deciding what she would say to Radio Man.

We were actually closer than I realized, and the house—as Horace had predicted—was impossible to miss. We braked and slid our way down a steep path and around one more switchback to the most beautiful cove yet—though one with nothing but rocks, no beach. On the far spit of land stood a tidy yellow house—two rooms, by the looks of it—with a bright red roof and a sliding glass door facing the water.

We picked our way from rock to rock around the little bay and then followed a sandy path to the door. Most visitors must come by boat, I thought. If he has visitors.

Ti-Anna took a deep breath, tucked her hair behind her ear and knocked on the sliding door.

Nothing happened. She knocked again. Nothing. Knock. Nothing. Knock.

Eventually, a curtain slid back a few inches, and a face appeared, atop a muscular body in a T-shirt, sweatpants and bare feet. The man stared down for what seemed like a long time. Then he unlocked the door and slid it open a few inches.

Ti-Anna bowed slightly and began talking in Chinese. The man listened. She talked some more. He didn't say anything. She talked some more. Finally, he answered. And closed the door. Locked it. Yanked the curtain shut.

"What did he say?"

She didn't answer. Instead she knocked again. And again. And again. Until the same thing: curtain, lock, door. He cocked his head. She said something. He said something. And closed the door. Lock. Curtain.

This time Ti-Anna turned around and sat on the cement ledge in front of the door.

"He said he won't talk with us."

Funny—I had guessed that much.

"And you said?"

"I said we were going to sleep on the rocks tonight, and come back and knock on his door in the morning. And that we'll do the same thing the next night, and the next morning. And every night, and every morning, until he does talk with us."

My first thought was, I'm going to be really, really hungry.

My second was, he doesn't know who he's messing with.

On the other hand, he looked as stubborn as she was. I wondered what my brother would think if I died on Lamma Island and he never got his backpack back.

I didn't say any of those things. I sat next to Ti-Anna, facing the lonely cove, and unwrapped a Snickers bar and gave her half. She took it without saying thank you. I ate it without saying I told you so.

Chapter 20

To say that what followed was the most uncomfortable night of my life doesn't say much. I'm not really the camping type, and all of my nights, to be honest, had been comfortable enough. But I think it's safe to say that even the hardiest camper wouldn't have been happy.

Fortunately, Ti-Anna didn't insist on sleeping on the rocks. I don't know how that idea had popped into her head. None of the rocks were big enough to stretch out on—and who knew what the tides would do during the night.

We picked our way back across the rocks in silence, with Ti-Anna leading the way and motoring fast. Back around the switchback, up into the woods, until you could barely hear the waves, toward the ruined house with the overhead fan.

I cleared my throat.

"How about here?" I said.

She looked dubiously at the house, and then even more dubiously at me.

"It's going to be dark soon," I said. "It may rain. Unless you want to try to find our way back to one of the villages, and see if we can rent a room . . .”

She shook her head at that idea, as I knew she would. Even out on Lamma, hotels would probably enter our passport numbers into some computer system.

The ruined house it was.

I don't want to dwell on that night. We got through it, though every time I looked at my watch, thinking an hour must have passed, only five minutes had crawled by.

It turned out the air mattresses were made to be inflated by something other than your mouth, so it took forever to blow them up. Which, given that we had all night to kill, maybe wasn't such a bad thing. But when they were ready, lying on them didn't feel much different from lying on the cement, except tippier. And it was starting to cool off, and of course we had nothing to cover ourselves with, and only an extra T-shirt to put on.

“So what are we going to do tomorrow if he still won't talk to us?” I asked calmly.

She answered with this: “When you bought all this candy and nothing to drink, what exactly were you thinking?”

A few minutes later, I asked, “Did you hear something?”

We did hear things, though to this day I don't know what. If you Google “Lamma Island” and “wildlife,” mostly what comes up are wildflowers. The things I heard definitely weren't wildflowers, and they weren't turtles, either. If they were Chinese security agents in suits and bad haircuts, I hoped they were uncomfortable too.

The worst of it, as I lay on that torturous air mattress imagining poisonous snakes slithering across the cement floor, was that for the first time since we'd left Washington I started really thinking about home again.

You know how things always seem worse at night? If you've said something mean to somebody, in the middle of the night it can begin to feel like the worst, most unforgivable thing that one friend has ever said to another, and when word gets around no one will ever speak to you again, and you wouldn't blame them. But then you wake up, and it's light outside, and you think, well, it wasn't all that bad. I'll just say sorry. And probably your friend doesn't remember the remark anyhow.

That's how this felt, except I had a lot worse to worry about than a mean remark. How could I have been so stupid as to think I could fool my brother into believing I was in New York City, when I was really halfway around the world? What if he had told our parents, and right now everyone was desperately looking for me? What if they called the police? And how could I ever repay this much money—assuming I ever got home, that is?

Most of all: Whatever made me think I had any business worrying about a Chinese democracy activist I had never even met? Crazy. You're crazy. That's what I kept helpfully telling myself, all night long. All that dark, hundred-hour night long.

I'm sure Ti-Anna tossed and turned through her own version of this, because when a gray smudge of dawn finally leaked into our ruined house, I looked over to her air mattress and found her as wide awake as I felt. And as unhappy.

We stood up, creakily, and walked to the edge of the clearing. Each of us, almost at the same moment, took a deep breath. The air was a mixture of sea-damp, rich soil, and some flowering tree unlike anything I'd ever experienced. Way off in the distance, you could hear the surf. A few gulls were doing wake-up cartwheels overhead.

Ti-Anna put a hand on my shoulder.

"Thank you," she said.

"I'm sorry I forgot the water," I said.

"And the coffee," she murmured. "Some toast with butter and jam would have been nice too."

"Do you think it's a coincidence that they built the hardest floor in Hong Kong right behind this guy's house?" I said.

"You mean, or did we just get lucky?" Ti-Anna answered.

We laughed. And when it turned out to be even harder to get the air *out* of the air mattresses than it had been getting the air *in*, that set us off again.

Finally, when we'd packed up what there was to pack up and eaten the last two granola bars, Ti-Anna said, as if answering my question from last night, "I know we can't stay in Hong Kong forever. When a week is up, we go home, no matter what, okay?"

It was the first time she'd ever hinted at the possibility that we might not find her dad.

"Well, maybe Radio Man is ready to talk," I said. I didn't see why he would be, but I wasn't going to say that.

"We have ways," Ti-Anna said, in a terrible German accent.

"You do that terribly," I said. She hit me, and we set off back down the hill.

Day Three: Tuesday

Lamma Island–Vietnam

Chapter 21

This time he slid open the door almost before Ti-Anna knocked. The same bare feet, sweatpants, T-shirt; the same muscles under the T-shirt. He stood aside for us to come in, with a couple of grunted words in Chinese, and then slid the door and curtain shut.

We found ourselves in a large, sunny room. Though the curtain was drawn facing the cove, to the right a bank of windows framed his spit of land and the open sea to the south. A low sofa and two mats with cushions were the only furniture. A barbell was in one corner, an open kitchenette in another. Through the kitchen window you could see his satellite dish. To the left was a door, closed. Presumably his computer and bed were behind it.

"Tea?" he asked.

"Yes, thank you," I said quickly, before Ti-Anna could interject.

"And some bread and jam?"

"No, thank you," Ti-Anna said even more quickly. I glared, but she refused to meet my eyes.

For a few minutes we balanced on the low couch while he busied himself with his kettle. When the tea had steeped, he poured us each a cup and then sat cross-legged on a mat facing us. His face looked tired, not unkind, but closed off in an odd way.

"I wish you had not returned," he said. He seemed to be looking at me as he spoke, and for some reason those were the last words he said in English, though apparently he could speak fluently enough. He turned to Ti-Anna and said something in Chinese, and off they went.

I don't want you to think it hurt my feelings to be shut out of the conversation. This was his country, and I was the one who had barged in without being able to speak the language. Why should he have to speak a foreign tongue in his own house? That was how I took it.

But it's harder than you might think to perch on a low, uncomfortable sofa while two people carry on a long conversation you can't understand. What's the polite thing to do? Watch them as they talk, as if you're following? That felt phony. Look out the window, as if you're bored? That felt rude.

I stared at my tea, really getting to know the bottom of that cup. I listened to the conversation, seeing if I could pick out any words repeating. (Not really; I couldn't even tell where one word ended and the next began.)

My thoughts began to drift. I wondered why he had let us in so easily this morning, after being so dead set against it the night before. I thought about the bread and jam sitting ten feet away, and willed it to levitate and float over to the couch. (No luck.) Eventually I closed my eyes. I have to admit, I may even have dozed. It's not like I'd gotten my usual eight hours.

What I know of the conversation, I had to piece together later from Ti-Anna as we hiked back up the island. But I don't think there's any point in making you wait like I had to. I can give you the gist right here.

Yes, he told her, Horace had it basically right: Ti-Anna's father had come to Hong Kong for the chance to meet with two labor leaders who wanted to meet him. They had gotten in touch through Radio Man, who had passed the message on to America.

"Not that I thought it would come to anything," he said, a little sourly, as Ti-Anna recalled it. "Democracy will come to China when it's good and ready; there's not much any exile can do to hurry it along."

He spat out "exile" like it was an insult, but then, wasn't he a kind of exile himself, living at the bottom of this little island? "But they asked me to pass a message, so I passed a message."

The sense Ti-Anna got was that Radio Man communicated with people inside China in codes, and in other ways he didn't want to talk about. He didn't know her father well, and he didn't think it was safe to send details via email. So her father had to come to Lamma for the specifics. He sat on the same couch where we were sitting now, got directions and left.

"And that's about all I know; I haven't heard from him since."

At that, he seemed ready to end the conversation.

"But what were the directions?" Ti-Anna asked.

"Honestly, it would be better for you not to know," he answered. "What can a couple of children do about any of this?"

Ti-Anna did not let herself show any anger. I certainly didn't hear her raise her voice. (Of course, maybe I was dozing.)

"Please," she said. "We haven't heard from my father since the day before he met with you. You are our last hope."

He sighed, and played with his cup, and sighed some more.

Finally, he said, "All right. I will tell you what I know. But please remember: I tried to warn you. You should go home. You are just children."

The meeting, he said, was to take place in Hanoi. If Ti-Anna's father still was determined, Radio Man could get a message inside China, and the meeting could take place five days later.

"Hanoi!" Ti-Anna said. ("Hanoi!" I said later, when she repeated this part of the conversation to me. "As in, Vietnam? That Hanoi? *The* Hanoi?")

The two men lived in southern China, Radio Man explained, and it was easier for them to slip across the long, mountainous border with Vietnam than into closely watched Hong Kong. He had a friend in Hanoi who could act as go-between.

"How can we call this man?" Ti-Anna asked.

"You can't," Radio Man answered. "It's too dangerous. Especially if something has gone wrong."

"Then we will go see him," she said.

He didn't like that idea at all, but she kept at him. Eventually he gave Ti-Anna an address in Hanoi, and a contact in Kowloon who he said could arrange visas and cheap airfare. And then he stood up, saying he had work to do.

When we were halfway around the cove, though, jumping one last time from rock to rock, we heard him calling. We turned to see him jogging after us, still barefoot, with a scrap of paper in his hand.

When he reached us, he handed Ti-Anna the paper, and spoke one last time in English.

"This is a friend in Hanoi," he said. "Please do not tell anyone I gave you her name. But I understand wanting to protect your family. She is a good person, and perhaps she may be of help if you go."

This big strong man looked strangely afraid to be out in the open. With one more glance at us, and a glance up the hillside, he turned and jogged back to his house. We watched until we saw the curtain slide shut one last time.

Chapter 22

It's amazing how two people can hear the exact same piece of news and have such different reactions.

Ti-Anna seemed energized by having discovered her father's next step, or what she assumed was his next step. She seemed to think this was the breakthrough we'd been waiting for. She could almost imagine that first hug.

Whereas I—well, at first I had a hard time even getting a clear story from her about what she had learned. She kept forgetting that I hadn't understood a word, and kept wanting to discuss what we should do next before I knew what he had said. And she was hiking so quickly that I had almost as much trouble keeping up with her walking as with her talking.

Not surprisingly, she led us toward a village on the other side of the island from where I'd meant for us to go. But it turned out there was a ferry from there back to Central, too, so it didn't really matter.

She was certain that Radio Man had given us great news, the missing link we'd been looking for. We knew where her father had been six days after his last contact with her and her mother, she said. All we had to do was find the go-between, and we'd find out what his next step had been. And if we got there in five days or less, we'd be gaining on him!

The more certain she sounded, the more dread I felt. Vietnam? That was a whole new proposition. It might look close enough when you're looking at a map of the world, but as I recalled, Asia was a pretty big continent, and going to Hanoi would take us farther away from Washington. Farther from home. For a second all my middle-of-the-night homesickness came flooding back, even though the sun was rapidly gaining on us and another fine day was hatching.

Instead of one of us not speaking the language and a lot of people speaking English, we'd *both* not be able to speak the language, and probably almost no one would speak English. And would my credit card do any good? Did Vietnam even have ATMs?

I had no idea. I didn't even know what Vietnam's money was called. I hadn't read the guidebook. I didn't *have* a guidebook. I didn't like the idea of going anywhere without a guidebook or local money.

"And we probably need visas," I said. "What makes you think we can get visas?"

"The same travel agent who can get us cheap flights can get us visas, too," she said impatiently.

She hadn't told me anything about a travel agent who was supposed to get us cheap flights. But I didn't stop to point that out. I figured she was talking about someone Radio Man had recommended.

"And why is he being so helpful with all this?" I asked.

"What's that supposed to mean?"

"Last night he wasn't going to talk with us, ever. Now he's helping us get visas into Vietnam? Why?"

She wheeled to face me.

"Maybe because he feels a little guilty about getting my father into this," she said. "Maybe because he'd like to know what happened too. Maybe he thinks my father is worth saving, and he thinks we can actually help—or have you ruled that possibility out, now that we're getting close?"

That was a low blow. But I can't say I really even heard it. I heard the words, but not so they really sunk in. I was following my own train of thought, hoping to catch her runaway engine.

"Ti-Anna, listen, even if your father did meet up with these labor leaders five days after calling you—"

"Six. One for him to get here, and then five more."

"Okay, six days after calling you. And even if this guy in Vietnam can tell us where they met—even so, a lot of days have passed since then. What do you think has happened since?"

She spoke in a flat, low voice that was scarier than any yelling could have been.

"I have no idea, okay?" I'd never seen Ti-Anna like this—white, and furious, and near tears all at the same time. "I have no idea. That's why I need to go and find out. That's why I'm doing this. If you're too scared to come along with me, fine. Just lend me the money for airfare. I promise I'll pay you back."

She turned and resumed marching toward Picnic Bay, which had come into sight below us.

"That is so unfair," I said, running to catch up to her. "You know I'm not going to let you go on alone. And yes, I am scared! You should be scared too! This is scary! Unless I'm very much mistaken, even Radio Man was scared, though I certainly couldn't guess of what."

At that, I have to admit, I was close to tears.

Ti-Anna stopped and turned back toward me again, but this time her face and body seemed to lose that tightness, and she was—she was herself again.

"Ethan, I'm sorry," she said. She hugged me, and for a while neither of us moved.

"Now I know what happens when you miss a meal," she finally said. I started laughing, which gave me the hiccups, which only made me laugh more. Which made her laugh. We were a mess.

She sat down on a wide tree root off to the side of the trail. You could see down to the little bay, where a few fishermen were paddling around their fish farms, which looked like square rafts, under which they hung cages of fish, which I figured eventually ended up in the restaurants, which we also could see, a ways up the beach. There were a few people sitting up that way, some at a café, one in the shade of a bamboo grove, smoking a cigarette.

"Look," she said. "You're right. I don't know what I was thinking. We have to figure this out together, and make our decision together."

I was still standing on the trail, and she looked up at me, squinting into the sun. "And if you think it's stupid to go, we won't go."

At which point I knew, of course, that we were going to Vietnam, if we could get there. From that point on I felt better about Ti-Anna. But the dread in the pit of my stomach—that didn't go away.

Chapter 23

The first ferry of the morning chugged into view, slowed toward the dock and threw its engines into reverse to ease into its berth. We boarded and took seats on the upper deck.

The people who'd been at the café got on right behind us. Then I noticed the guy who'd been squatting in the bamboo grove lift himself off his haunches, grind his cigarette butt into the dirt and stroll over to the ferry. Buzz cut, leather jacket; he stepped casually aboard as the gate closed.

I didn't say anything. Ti-Anna would chalk it up to imagination, hunger, fear. And maybe she'd be right. I didn't feel sure about anything anymore.

We watched Lamma Island get smaller and smaller and then closed our eyes, side by side, smelling the ocean and hearing the gulls. For a minute I tried to pretend everything was normal, and I got the feeling Ti-Anna was doing the same. If we get through this alive, I thought, I will come back to Hong Kong someday and ride this ferry for no reason but the fun of it. With Ti-Anna, hopefully.

Filing off at Central was like getting slammed back into the twenty-first century, back into the hubbub of bankers and students and office workers hurrying and scurrying from one important meeting to the next.

We headed toward the main Star Ferry pier. I was ready for breakfast; Ti-Anna was anxious to find the travel agent. As a compromise we'd agreed to take the ferry back to Kowloon and then get something to eat, before finding the office.

But an irresistible odor came wafting our way from a peddler's cart between the two piers.

I was about to make the case that a pre-breakfast snack of fried dough and hot soy milk would not violate the terms of our compromise when I saw the man in the leather jacket, strolling ten or twelve yards behind us.

There was something frightening about his face. When I tell you he had a scar through his upper lip and running up one cheek, I know you'll think I'm making it up. Cheesy, right? Maybe he got it at central casting with the leather jacket.

But what was chilling wasn't the scar. It was the stare. As in: I'm not going to pretend, and what are you going to do about it?

I got in line at the fried dough cart, to Ti-Anna's exasperation, but when I explained under my breath what I had seen—what I thought I had seen—she didn't make fun of my runaway imagination.

She glanced his way and said, "Let's find a bench and see what he does."

By now even I had stopped feeling hungry, but we bought our snack anyway and sat. The guy, his jacket now slung over one shoulder, sat a hundred feet away and watched us with contempt.

"Now what?" I said.

"Let's lose him!" Ti-Anna said. "We can't have him following us to the travel agent."

I almost wished she had dismissed my fears as paranoia.

"Okay, first of all, we're not positive he's following us," I said. Even as I said that, I knew it was wrong. The guy had lit a cigarette, cupping his lighter from the wind, and was eyeing us through half-closed eyes. "And second of all, how?"

"If he follows us onto the ferry, we'll know for sure," Ti-Anna said. "And we can hop off just as it's leaving."

We watched a couple of ferries load and depart. There was, in fact, no way to "hop off." Over the decades they had built this ferry into a pretty efficient system, and they tended to make sure the gate was closed before setting off.

These were big ships, almost like old steamboats, except without the paddle wheel. Two stories—green lower deck, white above—with eight lifeboats on top, inside decks, outside decks, the works.

"The only way," Ti-Anna mused after observing a couple of departures, "would be to climb onto that side and then jump back on the pier as it pulls out. Late enough so that he can't follow. And early enough so you don't fall in, of course."

My contribution to the plan: "You can't be serious."

It's not like the Star Ferry company had never thought of people doing this, and they obviously didn't think it was a good idea. There was a railing all along the pier, so there was in fact no place to jump to.

But she was serious, so we were serious, and so—off we went.

We each still had our Octopus cards—that's what they call their transit fare cards, for some reason. We tossed the fried dough into a trash bin and made our way through the throngs onto the ferry. I didn't look back but somehow I knew Leather Jacket was behind us. And then, sure enough, there he was. On board.

We stood near the side, and as the boat started pulling out we both hoisted ourselves onto the rail and—one, two, three—jumped.

Ti-Anna landed cleanly on the pier railing, balanced for a split second and jumped forward. I slithered down the outside, caught myself, but couldn't get a grip to climb back over.

For an instant I was frozen to the spot, the boat pulling away, the dark waves way beneath me. In that instant I saw Leather Jacket staring at me from the boat with a bone-chilling hatred, as if willing me to drop into the depths.

Then everyone was yelling, and Ti-Anna was pulling me up and over, and I was tumbling and picking myself up and running after her as fast as I could possibly run. Which was a lot faster than I had ever run before.

We didn't stop until we were off the pier and three or four blocks away. My heart was pounding so loudly I was sure the police would be able to track us by picking up the beat. Ti-Anna was bent over, hands on knees.

"You okay?" she gasped.

My palms were scraped, my pride was hurt and I was scared out of my wits. Otherwise I was fine, as far as I could tell.

She gave me a big grin. "I think we lost him," she said.

I couldn't believe we had pulled it off, but we did seem to be in the clear.

"Thanks for saving me," I said.

She shrugged. "I keep forgetting," she said. "You're not at your best before breakfast."

We agreed it would make sense to avoid the Star Ferry—preferably forever. Fortunately, Hong Kong's subway goes under the harbor, so we found a station and rode a few stops into Kowloon, getting off far enough from the harbor that we couldn't possibly bump into anyone who might be looking for us.

As we emerged up the escalator, the first thing we saw was a McDonald's. We walked in, no debate. Even Ti-Anna chowed down. I pushed thoughts of home from my mind.

Chapter 24

I felt better with a couple of Egg McMuffins in me—and, yes, they did taste exactly the same, though there were a couple of more intriguing things on the menu, like shrimp burgers and a burger with pork, cabbage and teriyaki sauce, which I promised myself I'd try the next time. If there was a next time.

I felt even better when right after breakfast we found a currency exchange store and got hold of some Vietnamese money—dong, they turned out to be called. And I felt better still when we found a bookstore with an English-language section not far from the currency store, and I bought an excellent guidebook to Vietnam.

"Nothing beats having a good guidebook in your backpack," I told Ti-Anna. "Except maybe having a good map."

She rolled her eyes. "I suppose it's preferable to a biography of a war-mongering American general who spent most of his life killing people who look like me, in one country or another," she said.

A low blow. But I let it pass, since I had, to be honest, been regretting having stuffed MacArthur in my pack. So far I hadn't had a lot of down time for reading.

We stopped at an Internet café, where we tried to find out something about the people Radio Man was sending us to. We didn't get a single hit for the guy he said acted as go-between for Ti-Anna's father, which gave me one more thing to be nervous about. What if he didn't exist, and Radio Man had made up some name just to get us off his back?

On the other hand, the woman he'd run onto the beach to tell us about, Anna Sydney, turned out to be real—an American running the Southeast Asia office of something called International Justice Mission, which, according to its website, helped people in poor countries where the local police often helped only the rich. They would try to rescue, or encourage the police to rescue, kids who got sold to work in salt mines or carpet factories or brothels. It sounded like noble work, though we couldn't figure why Radio Man would have given us the name of someone who seemed to have nothing to do with China.

We updated and reprinted our parental "permission" letters. They explained that we'd been delayed and were catching up to a school trip to Hanoi, and thank you for every courtesy. I know, there's no excuse for forging anyone's signature. But by this point, we were so past excuses for anything that I hardly worried about that.

Or, put it this way: I was worried about so many things that this one barely made my list. Had Ti-Anna's father really gone to Vietnam? What could have happened there to keep him from ever calling again? What would Ti-Anna do if we got to Vietnam and couldn't find out? Or found out, and the answer was something terrible?

That last one worried me most of all—a lot more than forging my mother's signature.

Of course, we didn't talk about any of that. We did what we needed to do, step by step.

We found the travel agent, if you can call her that, in what I guessed passed for suburbs in Hong Kong. It took us a long time to figure it out on the map, and even longer to ride to nearly the end of one of the subway lines. Then we had to walk past one big apartment complex after another, their balconies spilling over with plants and birdcages and bedding hanging out to air.

On the sixth floor of one of these buildings that looked like every other building was an apartment door that looked like every other apartment door: the address Radio Man had given us.

We knocked, heard some shuffling and words we couldn't make out. When I answered in English, a young woman with her black hair cut like a boy's opened the door a few inches. She was too short to look through her peephole.

It seemed an extremely unlikely place to buy airline tickets, let alone acquire foreign visas. I could hear a television in the background, and a baby. Ti-Anna explained what we were after, and the woman led us into her place as if people happened by all the time, wondering if there might be airline tickets for sale.

Her living room seemed also to be her dining room, office and, with a playpen smack in front of the television, nursery. Within half an hour she had sold us what she promised were tickets to Hanoi, departing from Hong Kong at five a.m. the next morning on an airline I had never heard of, and two letters which she swore we could exchange for thirty-day entrance visas when we landed in the Socialist Republic of Vietnam. All of which cost a lot less than I'd been worrying it would. She swiped my Visa card on a handheld machine she produced from behind an alarmingly cloudy fish tank.

We managed all this even though her English was almost impossible to understand, and her Chinese (Ti-Anna told me later) even less penetrable. The baby cried in its playpen the whole time, softly, never stopping but never getting more upset, either, as if it was used to waiting its turn.

The woman didn't ask why we were going, or why we were in

Hong Kong in the first place, or how we had found her, for that matter. When we were finished, she simply waved us to the door and went into her kitchen. We could hear the baby, still crying patiently, as we walked away.

Heading back to the subway, we debated what to do next. We could have used a shower and a change of clothes. At least, I could have. But having nearly killed ourselves (or at least, myself) to lose our shadow, it would have been stupid to go back to base and let him catch up with us again. For the same reason, we decided it would be safer not to get in touch with Horace.

So we moved from one coffee shop to another. I studied the Vietnam guidebook. Ti-Anna worked at reading a novel she'd bought in Chinese, which she said was good practice and would make her father happy. In the evening we rode the bus out to the airport, found a clean patch of floor in a quiet corner and took turns dozing, or trying to doze, until it was time to fly to Hanoi.

At immigration, no one even asked to see the letters from our parents: another masterpiece that would never see the light of day.

Day Four: Wednesday

Hanoi

Chapter 25

Once we managed to cross a street in old Hanoi, I felt more hopeful than I had in a long time.

The streets were narrow, and lined with shops with no doors or walls, spilling their goods onto what would have been the sidewalks—except there were no sidewalks, either.

And there were no traffic lights, or traffic policemen or stop signs or, as far as I could see, rules of any kind.

What there were: More mopeds, motorcycles and bicycles than you knew existed. Lots of them with two or even three people hanging on, sometimes hefting baskets of mangoes or giant containers of auto parts, all coming at us in an unending river of honks and bells and exhaust.

Ti-Anna and I stood at the corner, after the bus from the airport had deposited us, and thought: We will never get across. This is where our lives will end.

But here's the thing: You *can* get across. And the way you do it is by just . . . walking . . . across. Not too fast, not too slow: the key is, no unpredictable movements. The traffic never stops. It doesn't even seem to notice. But somehow, it flows around you. The motor-cycle drivers have to have faith that you're going to keep walking across that road, pretty much at the same speed you've *been* walk-ing across the road, and you have to have faith that they won't hit you. They might flow behind you, they might flow before you, but they won't hit you. You try not to catch their eye, either, or even really look at what's coming. That only confuses things. Instead, you just . . . keep . . . walking.

And when you get to the other side, you can't believe you've made it. Your blood pressure comes down a bit, and you think, Maybe there is hope. If a human being can cross that road while traffic never stops, anything is possible.

By afternoon, crossing the street wasn't the only reason I was feeling (foolishly, as it would turn out) a little better.

First of all, the tickets to Hanoi had turned out to be real. The airline seemed to be under the same management as the Rising Phoenix, in terms of comfort and service—I'll do you a favor and not describe the box "breakfast" they handed out along the way—but it got us there, no questions asked.

And when we arrived, Ti-Anna let me persuade her not to go straight to Radio Man's go-between—whose name, by the way, was Thieu. I'd been arguing that we were exhausted, having pretty much missed a night's sleep, and it would be more sensible to find a hotel, get cleaned up, maybe even buy a new T-shirt and find him the next morning. What difference could one day make?

She wasn't having any of it, at first. She was determined to gain ground on her father, as she imagined it.

But she gave in when we exited the Hanoi airport. The crowd there was like nothing you've ever seen—thousands of people yell-ing and shoving and looking for relatives and offering cab rides, in one frenzied, cacophonous (to us) mass. Anyway, it was like noth-ing *we'd* ever seen; it was Ti-Anna's first foreign country, really, since Hong Kong hadn't felt totally foreign to her. Plus, if Hong Kong had felt warm, this was *hot*—ninety-something with a drenching, deafening rain pouring onto the airport portico. (Did I mention that Vietnam's rainy season had begun?)

It took the wind out of us—even out of Ti-Anna. So we made our way to the old part of Hanoi, and we made our way across one street, and then another, and another, until we felt like pros, and we found a cheap hotel that wasn't too dirty, and we dried off and took a shower (and dried off again), and generally began to feel better.

And then, in slightly better shape, we found Anna Sydney.

The map showed her office to be not far from our hotel, so we took a chance on finding her in, as we had with Horace. We walked around Hoan Kiem Lake, where couples were strolling and rowboating in what was now a drizzle, and found her office on the fourth floor of a soot-stained old building a few blocks from the lake.

I wouldn't have been able to guess her age. Her skin was cracked and wrinkled, but more from being outside than from being old, and her short hair was between blond and gray.

She had the air of someone who generally knew what she was doing. Also of someone who was always busy. When we told her who had sent us, her eyes widened. When Ti-Anna explained, as briefly as she could, who she was, and why we were there, her eyes got even wider.

"But you're just children!" she said. Which, coming from her, felt more comforting than insulting.

And then: "You must be starving!" After which, needless to say, she could do no wrong in my book.

As we descended in her creaking elevator, she told us to call her Sydney. "Everyone does," she said. There had been three Annas in her kindergarten class, she explained, and somehow they became Anna 1, Anna 2 and Sydney.

"It broke my mother's heart, because she loved the name Anna, and she called me that until the day she died," Sydney said. "She was the only one who did."

She shepherded us across the street for a big bowl of pho bo, which are noodles that Vietnamese people seemed to eat at any time of day. Pho are the noodles in soup, and bo is beef, because you can get it with slices of meat on top. Like most restaurants we saw, the noodle place was open to the busy street, so it was hard to say whether we were sitting inside or outside, though a metal awning protected us from the clattering rain.

Instead of asking a lot of questions right away, like most grown-ups would have done, she let us ask her about what she was doing.

It might be hard to believe long after slavery had supposedly been abolished, she said, but in all these poor countries, there were people—especially young girls and women—being bought and sold. Burmese girls were sold as wives for Chinese men, Laotian girls were sold into prostitution in Vietnam, Vietnamese girls were sold into prostitution in Thailand.

Girls were made prisoners in their own countries too, she said. But if they were shipped across borders, to places where they didn't know anyone and couldn't speak the language, they had even less power to resist. If they didn't have passports, they might be afraid to run to the police. If they did run to the police, the police might sell them back.

Technically, slavery and prostitution were against the law in all these countries. Sydney's group tried to get police and prosecutors to make the laws more than theoretical. There was a lot of bribery and the criminal gangs were tough and well organized. But, she said, there were also people who wanted to do the right thing, including honest police officers. She'd been at it a lot of years, she told us.

That was how she had met Radio Man. One day years before he'd somehow heard about a group of young women who'd been taken from their villages in western China and shipped to a big city in eastern China—not to work as prostitutes, but in a factory where they were locked in their dormitories at night and charged more for dinner every night than they made in wages every day, so the longer they worked the more they owed. She was working in Hong Kong then, and he'd called her for help, and they'd been friends ever since, she said.

"But I've been worried about him lately," she said, without elaborating. "How did he seem?"

Not having anything to compare to, we weren't sure how to answer that question. Ti-Anna recounted how at first he'd sent us away, and how the next morning he had changed his mind, and how he'd come running after us on the rocks to give us Sydney's name.

She took that in for a minute.

"I suppose you know that he had to leave his family behind in China," she said. "I think that must make life awfully hard for him."

I thought about his nearly empty house, with a single barbell in the corner, and about his family back in China. It didn't make me feel more warmly toward the guy, but it did put things in a different light.

By this time we'd finished our noodles.

"Did you both have enough to eat?" Sydney asked.

"If Ethan ever tells you he's full," Ti-Anna said, "you'll know he's speaking in some kind of secret code."

Sydney laughed. "I'll try to keep that in mind," she said.

Since every little restaurant in Hanoi seemed to feature one thing and one thing only, we got up and moved a few shops down to a place that served coffee and pastries.

We found stools around a low round table on what would have been the sidewalk, if Hanoi had had sidewalks, and Sydney brought the conversation back to Ti-Anna and her dad.

113

She reacted to our story with something between amazement and horror.

"What I *should* do is put both of you on a plane this instant and send you right back home," she said.

Good luck with that, I thought, and, after taking one look at Ti-Anna's face, Sydney just sighed.

"Well, at a minimum I will go with you to meet this Mr. Thieu," she said, adding that she would bring a couple of Vietnamese friends along too.

That sounded good to me, but Ti-Anna (as I should have known she would) shook her head.

"I don't want to spook him," she said. If he had arranged a meeting for her father that the authorities didn't know about, he'd be more willing to tell her and a friend than a group including Vietnamese men he didn't know, she reasoned.

They argued back and forth, but in the end Sydney gave in. Vietnam was a Communist country, like China, and even though it didn't always get along with China, police in Hanoi might not have felt much more warmly about a democracy activist like Ti-Anna's father than police in his own country. Sydney said she couldn't disagree with that.

Though she didn't look happy about it, she helped us find his address on our map—it was north of the old city, not too far from Hanoi's other lake—and made us promise to let her know what happened.

"Do you have a phone that works here?" she asked.

I hadn't tried mine, but I was pretty sure it wouldn't. She took us back up to her office and lent us one.

"I'm number two on the speed dial," she said. "Call me!"

We promised we would. Then we went back to our hotel and collapsed.

As I lay in the dark, I calculated that it had been four days since we'd left home. I wondered if my parents were still in Geneva. I wondered if my brother had come by to water the plants.

And then, as tired from crossing Hanoi's streets as from spending the previous night on an airport floor, I dropped off to sleep before I could wonder about anything more.

Day Five: Thursday

Hanoi–Haiphong

Chapter 26

When I say Mr. Thieu looked like a rat, I don't mean to be insulting. Mr. Thieu just really looked like a rat.

We found his place without much trouble. It was odd—not a building right on the street, but a gate to a big plot of land. Big for Hanoi, anyway, where everyone seemed to live on top of each other. From the street you could see a jumble of greenery and, set back a ways, part of a red and black roof, almost as if an old temple had been converted into something else.

I pushed a buzzer in the wall.

Nothing happened.

"We could climb over," Ti-Anna mused.

The gate looked scalable, barely. But her suggestion was enough to make the scrapes on my palms start stinging again.

"Please," I said. "Enough jumping around."

I pushed the buzzer again, and almost instantly we heard the gate unlatch, as if Mr. Thieu had a rule not to answer unless someone buzzed twice.

He looked, as I said, like a rat: beady eyes in a puffed-up face, sharp nose, tufty hair that looked like he'd cut it himself, pink curly tail. No, just kidding; no tail. But you almost expected one.

Before Ti-Anna could get more than a sentence into explaining who had sent us, Mr. Thieu cut her off.

"I know who you are," he said, in heavily accented English. "Come back tonight. Alone."

"We are alone," Ti-Anna protested.

"No," he said, pointing to me. "You are not alone. If you want to hear about your father, come back tonight. Alone."

And with that he ducked away. The rusty metal gate swung slowly shut, with a creak and a click.

We stood there, too surprised to speak. In fact, you know the five stages of grief? I don't either, exactly, but I remember reading them somewhere, and in Ti-Anna's face you could see her cycling through the ones I remember. Shock. Depression. Anger. Finally— what would you call it?—resignation: "I guess I'll just have to come back tonight," she said. (Yes, I know that was only four. It's not like someone had actually died.)

"You will not come back alone," I said.

Thus began an argument that continued, in fits and starts, for the rest of that day.

Not that we stood in front of the gate all day. After a while, we turned around and sat in front of it, leaning back against the wall. Arguing. Then we started walking south, back toward downtown. Arguing. We stopped for some pho. Arguing.

As the tiresome day wore on, we walked and argued and walked some more. I would say, "I don't think you should go back alone." And Ti-Anna would say, "If that's the only way he's going to tell us where my father went, then I'm going." "You shouldn't." "Why not?" "Because."

"Maybe Radio Man didn't mention you, only 'the daughter,' and so he doesn't know whether he can trust you," Ti-Anna guessed.

"Maybe he's scared he'll get in trouble, and it's safer to tell one person than two. Maybe he doesn't like white people."

At some level, I'm sure Ti-Anna knew that none of those made much sense. But she had come this far, she felt like she was about to find out what had happened to her father, and she wasn't going to let anything stop her now. And *I* had come this far so she wouldn't have to do this alone, and *I* wasn't going to let anything stop *me*.

The rain was streaming down our faces, even as sweat was trickling down our backs.

To kill time, and get under some kind of roof, we visited Ho Chi Minh, though he happens to be dead.

Ho was the Communist leader who led Vietnam in wars against the French, in the 1950s and '60s, and against the Americans, in the 1960s and '70s, eventually beating both. According to their official history, which of course is written by the Communists who still run the place, he is the beloved father of his nation—their George Washington. Yes, just like the Chinese and Mao.

They have him pickled and on display, in this monumental mausoleum in the middle of a parade ground in the middle of Hanoi. (Yes, just like Mao in Beijing.) To see him you have to go through a metal detector and get in a long line, and there are guards telling you to take your hands out of your pockets and keep quiet. When you get inside it's like being inside a temple, or a funeral home.

While we were waiting to get in, I started in on the sickness of creating state religions around Communist dictators. Ti-Anna shushed me, and I thought back to the last time I was shooting my mouth off about a pickled Communist dictator. That seemed like a couple of eons ago.

I shut up. But as we filed past the mummified corpse, nicely turned out in a shirt and tie, I couldn't help nudging Ti-Anna and

121

whispering, "How do we know he's not made of wax?" Because, honestly, he looked suspiciously orange.

"Shhh!" she said again. "Not here!"

"Shhh!" a guard said, in a less friendly way.

When we got outside, we resumed our arguing. All I could think about was Rat-face, and why he didn't want me along.

"Look," Ti-Anna said, in what she obviously thought of as a compromise. "You can wait right outside the gate. He'll know you're there. What could go wrong?"

Which is the question that was echoing in my mind, over and over, as we headed back to Mr. Thieu's. Because, of course, Ti-Anna had won the argument and was planning to go in alone. I had agreed to wait right outside the gate.

Chapter 27

I might have kept my promise, too, if the gate hadn't closed so slowly.

We returned to the house as darkness fell. I hung back as Ti-Anna punched the buzzer. The gate opened, Ti-Anna disappeared, the gate swung back—and paused, for just an instant.

Without thinking—or maybe because in some corner of my mind I'd been thinking about it all day—I darted through the gap before the gate clicked shut, and dropped into the shrubbery.

Ti-Anna was being escorted up the path, through shadows. I assumed the man next to her was Rat-face.

I squatted in the humid Hanoi night, surrounded by cicadas even noisier than my ragged breathing. I had no plan. I couldn't have told you why I had done what I did, or what I thought I was going to do next, except that I didn't trust Mr. Thieu, and I didn't want a wall separating me from Ti-Anna.

I edged forward through an unkempt garden. The driveway opened onto a gravel-covered lot that encircled Thieu's house like a moat. It wasn't really a house, though—it looked more like a squat pagoda, with the ground floor lit up and the higher floors in darkness. An old army truck, with a canvas roof, was parked by the door.

Curtains were pulled across the windows. But as I crept along the edge of the gravel clearing, I noticed an outdoor wooden stairway connecting the porch to a second-floor balcony. I decided to make a run for it.

Every footstep was like an explosion on the gravel as I sprinted through the light. But I made it across and up the stairs. I listened, and let my breathing slow again. It didn't seem I'd been noticed.

They were talking beneath me, but I couldn't hear what they were saying, in part because the truck was idling noisily around the corner. Luckily its rumble covered the creaking of the wood floor, too, as I crept along the balcony.

A door opened easily, into a storeroom that took up the entire second floor—no furniture, as best I could make out in the bit of light that seeped in, just boxes and old file cabinets. From here, the voices were clearer—there was Ti-Anna speaking now, I was sure—but still indistinct. Then I noticed a bit of light, a small hole in the floor. I tiptoed over, lay flat and peered down: nothing. Angled slats made it impossible to see anything but the ceiling fan below. But pressing an ear to the opening I could hear almost as though I were in the room.

"I don't believe you," Ti-Anna was saying angrily.

"See for yourself," a man said. It did not sound like Thieu—the voice was deeper, the English less accented. He said something in Vietnamese, and I heard some walking and some rustling. "Here are the photos," he said.

Ti-Anna gasped. "My father."

"Yes," the man said.

"And who's that? The labor leaders?"

"She still does not get it," a different voice said. This was Thieu,

I was certain—the same higher-pitched, sneering rat voice we had heard at the gate that morning. "Stupid as her father."

"There never were any labor leaders," the other man said, in a more patient voice. "That was how they lured him here. Don't you see? Those are Chinese agents. Doing their job."

There was a pause.

"Where is he?" I heard Ti-Anna ask. Now she sounded more frightened than angry, as though she didn't want to hear the answer.

"Not our business," the man said. "But that car? From China. Probably they drove back across the border and threw him in prison that same day. If they'd wanted to kill him, they would not have had to go to such trouble." He laughed a bit. "Not to mention expense."

Now there was a longer pause. "So . . . why tell me now?" Ti-Anna asked.

"We were not supposed to," the man said. "But I think, why not? Where you are going now"—the blood froze in my veins—"you will not be telling anyone. So what harm in satisfying your curiosity?"

"You're going to kill me?" She sounded a lot more composed than I would have.

"No." There was a chilly laugh. "What a waste that would be— an attractive young woman like you. These men"—I heard something, and assumed he was thumping the photo—"want you out of the way. 'A good lesson,' they say. 'They will think twice about making trouble again, if they know even the children are not safe.' But they didn't tell us how. Now we will give you something to help you sleep. And you will go on a ride. And when you wake up— well, I don't want to spoil the surprise. You will have a new life, believe me."

The next second all hell seemed to break loose. Something was scraping along the ground, Ti-Anna was screaming, men were yelling in Vietnamese. Then I heard a groan from Ti-Anna. A thump. Quieter talking in Vietnamese. The front door opening.

The truck, I thought. With its engine rumbling.

I scrambled to my feet, ran out to the porch and around the corner. Below me two men were shoving Ti-Anna into the truck while a third supervised. She was limp.

The two haulers clambered after her and disappeared for a minute. Then they slid back out onto the gravel, said a few words to the third man and walked back inside. The third man rehooked the flap, tugged it to make sure it was fixed and started toward the cab.

I climbed onto the balcony railing. The truck's canvas roof was about six feet below me. I knew I could either jump and try to hold on or lose Ti-Anna forever.

I jumped.

Chapter 28

The next—what was it, two hours? three? four?—were the scariest of my life.

The tarp sagged when I jumped, but didn't give way. I started snaking toward the back, thinking I could swing inside, grab Ti-Anna and make a run for it. But as I hung my head over the edge, the truck lurched forward.

It was all I could do not to tumble off. I grabbed the edge of the tarp and managed to wriggle feetfirst, inch by inch, toward the front of the truck as it rumbled down the driveway.

When it stopped at the gate, I scooted back a couple more feet so I could loop my ankles under a rope that ran side to side near the cab. With my hands I grabbed hold of a parallel rope toward the back. I didn't dare let go long enough to turn around. As we lurched onto the street, I was backward, spread-eagled, facedown and scared out of my mind.

Right then, of course, it started to pour.

For a while I barely opened my eyes. The driver obviously had had a bad day. He braked hard, accelerated harder, ground his gears and careened around every corner. He seemed to aim the truck at every pothole he could find, and Hanoi's streets gave him plenty of chances. Rivulets of tropical rain gushed down the canvas. The rope was rubbing raw my scrapes from the pier.

But nothing lasts forever, right? That's what I kept telling myself. Just hold on. And eventually we had left the center of the city and settled onto a smoother, straighter roadway.

I opened my eyes, feeling like a fool for not having paid more attention. Now I knew we were heading out of Hanoi, but I had no idea which way.

Think, I told myself. You need a plan. What is your plan?

Everything was swirling in my head. Ti-Anna's limp body as they slung her into the truck. Rat-face's sneering *She still does not get it.* The dark concrete apartment blocks marching past me in the night.

The rain eased and I lifted my head slightly. We were on a two-lane divided road with few lights and little traffic. Every once in a while we'd flash through a commercial strip, where a few men would be squatting on low stools clutching bottles of beer. A store or two would be deserted but garishly lit—once, a store with nothing but vases; another time, nothing but stuffed animals.

At one intersection four men were playing Ping-Pong, outdoors, with a couple of kerosene lanterns to light their game. I wondered if I was hallucinating.

In my pockets I had my passport, some dollars, some dong, and the cell phone Sydney had given us. Not that I could get to it: There was no way I could let go of the rope, reach back into my pocket and pull out the phone without getting blown off and flipping end over end down the highway.

But even if we stopped, and I could get someplace where I could make a call without being overheard, what would I do? Punch number 2 and say, "Sydney, I'm on a truck, Ti-Anna's been drugged and kidnapped and she's inside, and, uh, no, I have no idea where. And no, I have no idea who. And as to why—"

I didn't want to think about why, about what they might have in mind for Ti-Anna, after some of the stories Sydney had told us. But what would she do with a call like that, anyway? What could she do?

And there was something else, too, which at first I didn't want to admit into my brain, but as time went on I couldn't keep it out. I had to figure out how this had gone so wrong. My first thought was that somehow *they* had followed us from Hong Kong to Hanoi, figured out where we were headed and gotten to the house before us. Rat-face wasn't the real Mr. Thieu, who we were supposed to meet, but some agent of the Chinese who'd been waiting to take Ti-Anna away.

Apartment buildings gave way to what I figured must be factories, hulking dark things behind imposing fences. As one after another whipped past, I had to admit there was another, maybe likelier possibility for what had gone wrong. If the conversation I'd overhead was what I thought it was, and the photos I hadn't seen were what I thought they were, then Ti-Anna's father had had the same rude surprise when he came to his meeting. He had been set up—and so had we, and fallen for it as he had.

The truck slowed, grinding its gears, and came to a stop. I pushed up, saw we were at a kind of toll gate and flopped back down, pressing myself into the tarp to become as two-dimensional as possible. I heard snatches of conversation, and then the driver lurched forward again. Still mad about something, I thought.

But if it was all a set-up, what did that mean? Was the original email to Ti-Anna's father the beginning of the plot, or had someone hijacked it along the way? Was it Horace? Or Radio Man?

And if Radio Man had intentionally sent Ti-Anna's father into a trap, and then Ti-Anna, too, what did that say about Sydney? After all, he'd sent us to her. All that business of her wanting to come with us, and worrying about us, and all the rest—had that been an act, part of this whole gruesome show?

The phone in my pocket began to feel more like an alien force than a means to rescue. If anyone was going to save Ti-Anna, it was going to have to be me.

As we drove on through the dark, with my hands bleeding and my feet numb, that began to seem like a bigger and bigger if. What could I possibly do? I wasn't sure I could even lift her out of the truck.

And if I did—then what? Carry her? Where? I had no idea where I was. It was hopeless.

Then I pictured, for the hundredth time, Ti-Anna's drugged body, bouncing on the floor of this army truck. Or maybe she was waking up now, in the dark, no idea where she was, or where I was, or what had happened or was going to happen.

I was furious at all of them—Horace, Radio Man, Sydney, Rat-face. I wasn't going to let them do this to her. One way or another, I wasn't going to let this happen.

I heard a cawing overhead, and realized it wasn't a crow but a seagull, and then I recognized something else: a salt tang in the air.

There, I thought, there's one good thing: now I know which direction we've been traveling: east. East out of Hanoi, toward the ocean—toward the Gulf of Tonkin.

I lifted my head to look for waves, or beach, or something. All I saw was darkness.

Day Six: Friday

Haiphong–Hanoi

Chapter 29

I was beginning to think I'd been wrong when I'd told myself that nothing can last forever. This truck was going to drive on and on through the rain and the dark, never stopping—only I wasn't going to be able to hold on forever. My hands would give way, my feet would unhook, I'd tumble onto a wet Vietnamese highway, and the truck—and Ti-Anna—would disappear into the night.

But then—could it be?—we weren't going quite as fast.

I lifted my head again. The road had narrowed, and looked deserted. The buildings were smaller, houses or shacks or little warehouses, I couldn't tell. There were no streetlights, and I could barely see beyond the pavement. I thought maybe I heard waves, but then I thought maybe I was imagining it.

Then, miracle of miracles, we really were slowing. Third gear, second gear, turn. Stop.

With the engine idling, the driver called out, got no response, called again. A voice responded, and the truck eased off the road and onto a graveled parking area, rolling another twenty yards or so before falling blessedly silent. It was an amazing relief not to have air rushing past.

It was also terrifying: suddenly I felt totally exposed. I held my breath and willed myself to be invisible.

The cab door opened and then slammed shut. There was some scraping on the gravel—rubbing out a cigarette butt?—and then a few steps and a knock on a door. A door opening, another hurried conversation, a door slamming shut. And then—quiet.

A light drizzle was tapping the roof of the cab, and now I was sure I could hear the rhythmic lapping of waves not far away. And that was it. No voices, no cars. Nothing.

Slowly, slowly, I uncurled my fingers from the rope and rolled stiffly onto my side.

We were parked in front of a low, long building, with ten or twelve windows facing our way. Two windows were lit, and enough light leaked out through grimy curtains to show that we were in a compound, framed by sheds and shacks and a couple of other low buildings like the one that had swallowed the driver.

An odd assortment of boats and vehicles and equipment was scattered around the lot: a truck like the one beneath me, a few motorcycles, a three-wheeled bicycle rickshaw, an old fishing boat listing to one side and ropes and crates and other junk I couldn't make out in the gloom.

I sat all the way up and rubbed my feet. Beyond those two windows the compound looked deserted, but I knew at least one other person was out there. I had to hope he—the guy in the gatehouse—had fallen back asleep.

I looked at my watch, which I had never adjusted. Back home it was three in the afternoon. Here it was eleven hours ahead. Two in the morning. Still plenty of darkness to come. Another good thing, I told myself.

Gingerly, I turned myself around, like a dog looking for the right position for a nap, and crawled toward the front of the truck. My muscles creaked and complained but they did what I told them to do. I figured eventually even my feet would feel normal.

I slid onto the roof of the cab and swung down, my feet finding the driver's open window and then the narrow running board and, finally, the ground.

I peered inside the cab, not knowing what I was looking for. It's not like you're going to find a map with an X drawn over our final destination, I told myself. There were no keys, either, just a crumpled cigarette pack and a lighter.

I grabbed the lighter and tiptoed toward the back of the truck. No one came running at me from the office building, or from the gatehouse.

I heard an odd snuffling inside the truck. Please, let her be okay, I thought. I unhooked and lifted the flap. In the darkness I could make out nothing, so I flicked the lighter and—I couldn't help it— let out a gasp.

Chapter 30

I'd been imagining Ti-Anna lying in empty darkness, maybe tossed on a few empty sacks. What I saw was the opposite of emptiness. Three rows of rope hammocks ran the length of the truck. Each row was triple-decked, one hammock on top of another on top of another. And in every hammock a girl, curled up to fit the tiny space.

In my shock I let the lighter close. I took a deep breath, hoisted myself into the truck and, with my hand shaking, flicked it on again. The flap closed behind me.

I had to turn sideways to slide between the rows. Some of the girls stared at me, in a vacant way. Some didn't bother. Some had blindfolds on. Some had tape over their mouths. None of them made a sound. There was a sour smell to the air.

I sidled up one narrow aisle, holding the lighter over one stack of hammocks after another. The girls were just that, most of them—girls; kids, really, though there were a few young women too. All were barefoot. A few had bruised faces or black eyes. None of them was Ti-Anna.

She's got to be here, I told myself. I saw them put her in. I would have seen them take her out. I sidled back toward the flap and pushed up the other row, flicking the lighter more and more impatiently until—there she was, in a hammock near the front, in the middle of a stack: one girl above her, one below.

I held the lighter close to her face. Her eyes were closed, but she looked unhurt, and she was breathing. Okay, I told myself. She's alive. Another good thing.

I shook her lightly and whispered her name. Her eyes flickered open. I moved the lighter nearer my face, so she could see me. For the longest time she stared almost uncomprehendingly, as if she were swimming up from somewhere deep, deep underwater. Then she reached out and touched my chest.

"You're soaking," she said.

"That's true," I whispered. I was so happy I wanted to squeeze her in my arms. She's okay, I thought. That's all that matters. We'll get out of this somehow. "It's the rainy season here in the Socialist Republic of Vietnam, in case you hadn't noticed."

"Where are we?" she said. She lifted her head and moaned, fell back down and asked again, more insistently. "Where are we? What is going on?"

"You were drugged," I said. "Do you remember going to Thieu's house? They injected you with something, and put you in this truck, and drove you toward the seashore. We've got to get you out of here. Fast."

Some of the other girls were watching us now, still without emotion, without curiosity, or maybe they were too scared to show either. Ti-Anna didn't seem to notice them. She closed her eyes again, and I closed the lighter; I didn't want to use it up. I couldn't see my hand six inches in front of my face.

I perched on the side of Ti-Anna's hammock, without putting my weight on it, and felt for her shoulder.

Then I heard her voice in the darkness.

"I do remember," she said. "They showed me pictures of my father. Ethan, he's alive! We have to— Ow! My head is pounding."

She had tried to sit up again, too fast. But this time she kept coming, more slowly, holding on to my arm and swinging her legs onto the ground.

"We have to get those photos, Ethan. Then *they* will have to admit he's alive, that they kidnapped him. Then they'll have to let him go." She paused. "God, it's like someone has a hammer inside my head. What do you think they gave me?"

"I don't know," I said. I didn't know whether to be cheered or terrified that Ti-Anna, a prisoner about to be sold into slavery, was confidently making plans to defeat the People's Republic of China.

"But listen to me, Ti-Anna. One thing at a time. We've got to get out of this truck. It could drive off again at any minute, God knows where. There's men all around, and they probably have guns." That was a guess, but it didn't seem unreasonable. "Let's see if you can walk."

I flicked the lighter one more time, and this time Ti-Anna noticed the girls. She looked above her, below her, all around, and I could see her taking it all in: the bruises, the naked feet, the taped mouths.

"My God," she breathed.

"Yes," I hissed. "I know. But we have to move, *now*."

She let me help her into a standing position and lead her toward the back.

I pushed the flap open a crack. After the blackness of the truck the lot seemed positively bright. No one was in sight.

I jumped down and turned to help Ti-Anna, who surveyed the inside of the truck one more time and then slid warily to the ground. We headed toward what looked like an empty shed as far from both the gatehouse and the lighted windows as we could get.

As Ti-Anna hop-stepped across the gravel, I understood why every girl was barefoot; it made it that much harder to escape. She winced with every step, and I was sure that with every wince her head pounded. But she kept up without complaint until we had collapsed on a pile of foul-smelling nets inside the shed.

We caught our breath.

"Ethan," Ti-Anna said as another mystery dawned on her. "How did *you* get here? How did you know I was here? How did you find me?"

"It's a long story," I said. "Let's get out of here, and I'll tell you all about it."

I looked nervously through the dirty window.

"We could use that pedicab," I said. "You can ride while I pedal. We have at least two hours of darkness left. If we can get past the guardhouse, we could get pretty far before they notice you're missing."

We were sitting thigh-to-thigh on the nets, and I could sense her mulling over what I'd said, and then I could sense her shaking her head, no, in the darkness, and somehow I knew what was coming.

"Ethan," she breathed. "We can't leave those girls. We just can't."

Chapter 31

We sat in the dark, breathing in Eau de Decayed Shrimp, while I let that sink in. I wasn't surprised, as I said. I didn't even disagree.

I just didn't see how we could save those girls.

Eventually, I said so.

"I know," Ti-Anna said softly. "I don't have a clue either. But—do you still have the phone?"

I knew where she was heading. As quickly as I could, I sketched out why I wondered whether we could trust Sydney.

Ti-Anna didn't respond for a while—for so long that I began to think maybe the drug had kicked in again or, worse, that she was giving up. I realized that the only thing scarier to me than Ti-Anna determined to rescue a hundred slave girls on the way to liberating her father would be Ti-Anna deciding that something was impossible.

"So," I finally said. "I know it's horrible, but—should we try the pedicab? Those guys won't hesitate to kill you if you piss them off, I'm pretty sure of that."

She still didn't answer.

Then, as if she hadn't heard my last comment at all, she said, "Here's what I think. You're right about Radio Man. I think he agreed to trick my father into this trip. Remember what Sydney said about his family back in China? Who knows what they threatened *him* with.

"But—here's the thing, Ethan: I'm sure he didn't want to. At least, he didn't want to do this to me—maybe with my dad there's some history we don't know, but he didn't want to do this to me. To us."

She paused, looking at me in the gloom. "That's why he sent us away at first; he had some idea of what they might make him do, if he let us in, but they didn't know we were there, so they hadn't sent him orders yet, so he tried to act as though it hadn't happened. That in itself took courage.

"By the time we showed up again the next morning, they had tracked us somehow—they would have known we hadn't gone back to your dump of a hotel." My dump? I thought. "So when we knocked on his door, he had to let us in. He had to do what he did.

"But he felt bad about it. I know he did."

It made me nervous to hear her assure me how certain she was, as if she was trying to convince herself.

But maybe she was right. "So because he felt bad, he came running after us with Sydney's number—outside, where *they* couldn't hear," I said. "As a good-luck charm."

"Maybe it was something he did so he could feel a little better about himself. 'I tried to save them,' he could tell himself," Ti-Anna said. "But it wasn't just a good-luck charm. Think about it. She really might have saved us, if I hadn't been so stupid and stubborn."

I pulled the phone out of my pocket and turned it on. What's the worst that could happen? I thought as I waited for it to power up.

Well, I answered myself, that's a no-brainer: As soon as she talks to you, she'll call whoever is sitting in that shabby little office across the boatyard, and they'll come get us both, and inject us with whatever they had drugged Ti-Anna with last time, only more of it.

And what if Sydney wasn't part of the plot? Even then, what good could she do us, or those girls? I knew we were somewhere along the ocean, but I didn't know where. Vietnam's coastline was at least a thousand miles long. That left a lot of room for guesswork.

Having run through all the reasons it made absolutely no sense to be doing what I was doing, I punched number two.

She answered on the third or fourth ring, sounding sleepy but on top of things as usual.

"Ti-Anna?" she said.

"No, it's Ethan," I said as loudly as I dared. "They tried to kidnap Ti-Anna, and they have a truckload of girls, and—and we don't know what to do. We're a few hours from Hanoi, next to the ocean, but I don't know where."

"You're about five kilometers north of Haiphong," Sydney said, and my blood ran cold. I covered the phone and whispered to Ti-Anna, "I told you! She knows where we are!"

Ti-Anna whispered back, "The phone probably has GPS," and at the same moment, as if she could hear my whisper, Sydney was saying, "Ethan, all our phones have locators. We need it for our work."

"Oh," I said.

"Where is Ti-Anna now, Ethan?"

"She's right next to me," I said. "I got her out. But all the others are in the truck, and we have no idea when it might drive off again, or how to stop it from going."

"And where are you, exactly?"

"In a shed. Still in the compound."

"Okay, listen to me," Sydney said, sounding all of a sudden very serious. "The single most useful thing you can do right now is not get yourselves killed. Do you understand? Probably they are going to put the girls on a boat and get them out to sea before daylight.

143

There's a terrific Haiphong police inspector whom I will call right now. She may be able to get some people there in time.

"If she does, you stay out of their way. And if she doesn't—you *still* stay out of the way, do you hear what I'm saying? And keep Ti-Anna out of the way. Do you hear me? These guys will not be playing."

I nodded. That didn't do Sydney much good, so I said, "Okay. Try to get them here fast." She clicked off without bothering to answer.

"What?" Ti-Anna said. I told her everything Sydney had said, and then for a while neither of us said anything.

I knew Sydney was right. Even more—I thought that once they noticed an empty hammock, they'd come looking for us, and so I was being unforgivably stupid not to get her out of the compound now.

But . . . Sydney hadn't seen those girls, curled up so still and terrified on their hammocks. Maybe she was right, there was nothing we could do. But walking away seemed, somehow, impossible.

We stayed, telling ourselves that we were waiting for the police, but really not knowing what else to do. I realized how exhausted I was. I might even have dozed off. Ti-Anna closed her eyes too.

At some point we were both awake and, in bits and pieces, began to fill each other in. I told Ti-Anna how I had snuck past the gate of the house in Hanoi, and what I had overheard of her conversation, and how I had jumped on top of her truck and stayed on top through the ride here.

"That was really dumb," she whispered. "You could have been killed." Then she leaned over and kissed the side of my forehead and said, "Thanks, Ethan."

We were both quiet for a few minutes and then Ti-Anna whispered, "Do you think all Vietnamese fishing nets are this stinky?"

"You mean, or did we just get lucky?"

She smiled, fleetingly. But soon she was thinking again about what she had learned inside the pagoda. She recounted the part of the conversation I'd missed and described the photos of her father being led away, the painful expression on his face, a mix of astonishment and fury and, most of all, she said, wounded pride.

"He must have known by then that he'd fallen into a trap, and I'm sure he hated himself for it," she said.

"If he fell into a trap, it was only because he so much wants the right thing for China," I said. "You have to admire that, not blame him."

That was when we heard the engine. At first, I thought, They've come! The police!

But then I knew what we were hearing. It was no paddy wagon, but the diesel engine of a boat coughing to life.

Chapter 32

For a minute, for some strange reason, the *thump-thump-thump* of the engine brought back a fifth-grade trip to the Eastern Shore, when we were studying the Chesapeake Bay. I closed my eyes and could smell the sunscreen my mother had made me put on. I wondered if Ti-Anna had taken the same trip.

"Ethan," she said.

I opened my eyes. She was standing over me.

"I'll go see what's happening," I whispered.

"I'm coming."

I shook my head.

"You can't move fast enough," I said, pointing to her feet. "I'll scout it out, and I'll come right back."

"Promise."

"I promise."

She helped yank me up, then followed me to the door. The courtyard was unchanged. The same light seeped from the office windows; there was no sign of life in the guardhouse; the truck was a dark, silent bulk.

If I turned right out the shed door and kept to our side of the courtyard, I thought I'd be able to slip between buildings and reach the bay.

I patted my pockets. Phone, passport, lighter.

"You keep this," I said, handing Ti-Anna the phone. "I'll be back in a minute."

And I would have been—I really meant to hold to my promise—if I hadn't tripped over that canister of gasoline.

I kept to the shadows of the outbuildings along the courtyard. The rain was taking a break, but a sharp, salty wind had picked up, and somewhere I could hear a loose line swinging against a metal pole.

A narrow passageway took me to the harbor. It did not resemble what I remembered of the Eastern Shore. There were docks and boats, but there was also junk everywhere: wooden boards, chipped buoys, rotting fish, crab shells. If a harbor could be a slum, this was a slum.

It wasn't hard to find where the sound was coming from. Bobbing gently at the end of a wooden dock thirty or forty feet out from the cement seawall was a fishing boat with black smoke belching out the back. It was substantial—plenty of room in the hold for human cargo, I thought. Its running lights were the only sign of life in the harbor.

I started making my way north on the seawall, alongside the low building. I knew I should go back and tell Ti-Anna what I'd seen. There was nothing I could do, except get caught. But I kept thinking about the girls. Would the gangsters carry them to the boat, I wondered, or make them run barefoot?

I'll just get a better look, I told myself. Maybe if I can read the boat's name, that will help.

Two windows were lighted on this side of the narrow building too, but since they had no curtains and, judging by how clearly the voices came through, no glass, I didn't dare look in. At least three people seemed to be talking, in a language I didn't recognize—not Vietnamese, I was pretty sure, but not Chinese either.

I dropped below the windows, crawled past and inched along until I could read the name of the ship. *Abella,* it said, with a little Filipino flag. Well, maybe that will be something to go on, I thought. And then I really was about to turn back, when I nearly fell over the fuel can.

I'm not sure how the idea came to me, but I swear all I had in mind was creating a diversion. I thought if I could get something burning, the boat would have to move to a different pier before they could load the girls, and maybe that would give Sydney's police inspector enough time.

I hefted the canister. It was full. I didn't know much about marine fuel, or about arson for that matter, but I could tell it held a lot of gallons. I lugged it to where the dock met the cement.

At first I thought I'd pour it all right there, and hope the fire would travel out along the dock. But the wood was damp, and the wind was shifty but mostly coming in from the sea. So I walked out as close to the boat as I dared and then turned the thing over and started shaking fuel on the wood as I walked slowly backward toward land.

Which leads me to my one piece of advice: if you're ever considering committing arson in the middle of a black and windy night, don't walk backward. I backed right into a pole, and started to slip on the wet wood and lost control of the canister, which fell onto the dock with a thud. A gray-haired man emerged from the boat's cockpit.

I flattened myself on the wood, trying to make myself two-dimensional yet again. After a minute the man retreated into his slave ship. I stood back up, lifted the canister and shook out the last drops.

My first few flicks of the lighter accomplished nothing. The wood wouldn't light. The air was cool by now, but I was beginning to sweat, certain that at any second the men would emerge from the office and find me kneeling there. I thought, maybe arson is harder than it looks in the movies. Maybe I better give up.

But then, slowly, almost lazily, a curlicue of flame sprouted from a wet board. It smoked, it sputtered, it came back to life—and suddenly it began to spread. One board, two boards—and then it was dancing. I took cover on the cement walk, behind a pile of nets.

I must have poured more gas nearer the boat, or it had had longer to soak in, because as the fire made its way outward it grew stronger and higher and brighter. It was almost mesmerizing, the way it hissed and crackled, and even though I knew I should be getting out of there, *right now*, before the men came running, I couldn't tear myself away.

Within a couple of minutes the fire was roaring. Try carrying your criminal cargo of innocent girls over those boards now, I thought.

Soon the boat captain was back out on his deck, shouting. Guess you'll have to swim to shore, I thought, feeling pleased with myself. I heard yells from the building. The fire leapt and started licking the boat itself. And that's when the world blew up and came to an end.

Or at least, it felt that way. I can't really say I saw the explosion, and I don't even remember hearing it. All I can say is I felt a force and a scalding heat and something like an overwhelming redness that was louder and brighter and more terrifying than anything I could have imagined. It sent me flying and knocked me flat on my back. And then everything went dark.

Chapter 33

Later, I realized that the boat must have been loaded with enough fuel to ship the girls a long way, so it didn't take much of a spark to blow it to smithereens. But that wasn't my first thought as I came back to consciousness.

I wondered what I could be lying on that was so hard and wet. I wondered why everything was so black. Then I opened my eyes. That helped.

Three men were standing in front of the office, arguing and gesturing toward the water. I noticed one of them had his belt buckle undone. I closed my eyes again and wondered why he had forgotten to do up his pants.

I heard a crackling, and realized it was fire, and remembered everything: that I was lying on my back on a wet cement seawall north of Haiphong, and that a fire was crackling because I had lit it, and that if I didn't want to get thrown into it I had better not let those guys see me.

I started to push up from the ground and— Ohh! Pain shot through my right leg. My head clunked back to the cement.

When the throbbing eased, I tried again, slowly, lifting my head a few inches. The dock was gone: a few charred pilings poked up. What had been the boat was a twisted mess of wood and other odds and ends, still burning, but without much intensity, as if the fire knew it had won and was getting bored.

Out to sea, there was the faintest line of pink in the sky. The men, close enough so that bits of their conversation wafted over me, were arguing.

Closer in my line of vision was a giant wooden spool, the kind that holds cable, and this giant spool happened to be perched on top of my leg. It was helping to hide me from the thugs, if they looked this way, so I thought maybe I should leave it be.

Then another bolt of pain charged through me and I changed my mind.

Summoning all my strength, I managed to shove the thing to the side. To this day I am positive that I screamed with pain and I can't explain why the thugs didn't look over. But they didn't. I lay back down. I think I would have passed out, except that I remembered the boat captain. And while I was wondering what had become of him, I had an even more terrible thought: Where were the girls?

Suddenly a vise was squeezing my chest. It couldn't be, I told myself. You would have heard them being taken off the truck.

Oh, yes? I answered myself as the vise squeezed harder. How about while you were dozing in the shed? You have no idea whether anyone was still in that truck. You might have—

Ignoring the pain, ignoring the thugs, I forced myself to my feet—or to my foot, since there was no way I could put any weight on the leg that had been pinned. I hopped past the end of the office building toward the courtyard, not even thinking of the men any longer, praying please, please, please, let them not have been on the boat. Please.

As I rounded the corner I could make them out in the early gray light: the girls. Ti-Anna was helping them out of the truck, one by one, and sending each one silently across the stones to our shed. That was when, I admit, I think I started to cry—out of relief, and gratitude, and then pain and fright and whatever chemicals a broken leg can send squirting through your body.

I had hopped halfway toward the truck before Ti-Anna saw me. She came running over and grabbed my hands. "I thought you were dead," she whispered.

"I'm sorry," I whispered back. "I thought all of them might be dead. All I meant to do was burn the dock, so that . . ."

She was staring at me, not hearing my words.

"What's happened?" she said. "You're all clammy. And"—she leaned in again—"that smell!"

"I think it's just burned hair," I said. I recognized the odor from chemistry lab. "And I might have broken my leg."

I leaned on Ti-Anna's shoulder and we started toward the truck. A group of girls was waiting patiently.

"When I heard the explosion, I thought I better get them off the truck, so they couldn't just be driven away again," Ti-Anna said. "At least this might slow things down."

"Still no police?"

She shook her head.

"Look what I found, way at the back."

Leaning against the tire was a plastic bag crammed with flip-flops and sandals and slippers. How thoughtful: they'd be ready to begin their slave labor as soon as they got to wherever they were going.

I don't know how Ti-Anna had persuaded the girls to listen to her, but now she hoisted herself into the truck and resumed her shepherding. As each girl prepared to jump off, Ti-Anna handed her a pair of shoes—I noticed Ti-Anna was wearing pink flip-flops with little yellow flowers—and directed her across the courtyard.

Finally, every hammock was empty. Ti-Anna climbed down and

refastened the tarp. We hobbled after the girls, with me leaning on her shoulder.

"How's your head?" I whispered.

"Better," she said.

Now that I knew I hadn't murdered a boatload of innocent young women, the pain from my leg came flooding back, and I thought I might pass out again.

There was barely space to sit in the shed, but a few wide-eyed girls silently made room. Ti-Anna eased me onto the nets. I felt a wave of nausea from the stench of rotting fish and the closeness of a hundred girls who had been treated like livestock.

When Ti-Anna pulled out the phone, I managed to croak out an objection.

"Ethan, if the police are coming, we'd better let them know what to expect—how things have changed since you talked to Sydney."

"Well, okay, but—well, don't tell her how the fire started," I said. She looked at me quizzically.

"There was a guy on the boat," I whispered, looking away as I told her.

She lowered the phone and slid down onto the nets, so we were sitting side by side.

"Maybe he jumped off in time," she said softly.

"Maybe," I said, and hoped it was true. I couldn't be sure it wasn't, though given the suddenness of the explosion I didn't think much of his chances.

"Ethan," she persisted in the same soft voice. "You did the right thing. You may have saved a hundred girls from horrible lives—and pretty short lives, for a lot of them."

I nodded and closed my eyes and heard her say, "But only if the police get here soon, before those monsters realize their truck is empty. Where are they?"

She made her call then, and explained what she could to

Sydney. I heard her say, "Yes, and we're going to need an ambulance too."

And then—I can't say if it was right away, I was losing track of time, but it seemed that way—there were odd two-tone sirens heading toward us, and lots of lights and noise. I thought I saw a Vietnamese woman wearing a Dallas Cowboys ball cap staring down at me, and figured I had passed from confusion into total hallucination.

Then someone was doing something to my leg, and someone else was poking my arm. My last thought, before I passed out, had something to do with how upset Ti-Anna had been when she thought I was dead.

Chapter 34

When I opened my eyes, Ti-Anna was perched on the edge of my bed.

"Finally," she said.

"Sorry," I said, or tried to say. I cleared my throat and tried again. "How long have you been sitting there?"

She smiled. "A while."

I was propped up in a single bed in a small room, very white, very clean. Leaves outside the window—we must be on the second or third floor. Whitest of all was my leg, with a cast from thigh to ankle. My palms were bandaged, and a couple of gauze pads were taped to my arms. But no tubes—that seemed like a good sign.

I found myself wondering whether you could get pho bo in a hospital in Haiphong.

"How's your head?" I asked.

"You asked me that already," Ti-Anna said. "It's fine."

Then I noticed a little girl sitting on a chair in the corner, absolutely still. She was holding a rag under one arm, and staring at Ti-Anna.

"Who's that?" I whispered.

"One of the girls from the truck," Ti-Anna said. "She won't let me out of her sight."

"She looks like she can't be more than nine or ten."

Ti-Anna nodded. "I know. Though Sydney says she could be a malnourished thirteen."

"Monsters," I said. Had Ti-Anna used that same word not long ago, or had that been part of some nightmare?

I lay back and closed my eyes. I noticed that my back was sore, I supposed from being thrown onto the seawall.

"Why is she holding that rag?" I whispered.

"You don't have to whisper," Ti-Anna said. "She doesn't understand English. It's her doll."

I opened my eyes. The girl was still staring at Ti-Anna. I guessed if you looked really hard, you could imagine the rag was a doll.

What monsters, I thought once more.

"So how do you feel?" Ti-Anna asked.

"Hungry," I said. "I wonder what you have to do to get breakfast around here."

"You slept through breakfast," she said. "And quite a bit more. Are you up to talking with Inspector Tranh? She wants to ask you a few questions."

Before I could answer, an older Vietnamese woman wearing a Cowboys ball cap walked in, with Sydney right behind. So it hadn't been a hallucination.

Ti-Anna put her hand on my arm and whispered, "Don't worry." Sydney introduced the inspector, who thanked me.

"This is a gang we've been trying to stop for a long time," she said to me, in English that was only lightly accented. "They always managed to stay one step ahead. Until you and Miss Chen led us to them."

She noticed me eyeing her cap.

"You are from Redskins territory, if I am not mistaken, Mr. Wynkoop," she said. "Does my cap offend you?"

The truth is I've never been one of those I'm-from-Washington-so-I-have-to-hate-Dallas people, but she seemed so delighted at the idea of offending me that I didn't want to disappoint her.

"I'm not a big Cowboys fan," I admitted.

"Too bad," she chortled.

She said the gang had been moving girls from Laos and Cambodia into Vietnam and beyond, but always taking different roads and leaving from different little harbors, disappearing before police caught wind of the latest shipment.

"The girls you helped rescue were from Laos, and they are on their way home," she said.

"Why not her?" I asked, pointing to the girl who was now clutching Ti-Anna's hand.

"She was reluctant to separate from Ti-Anna," Sydney explained, "so the inspector let them both ride with you in the ambulance to Hanoi. We're trying to find a relative in Laos to come fetch her."

"Hanoi?" I said. Now I was really confused.

Inspector Tranh jumped in. "When the emergency technicians were able to stabilize you last night, we decided, after some conversation with Ms. Sydney, to transport you here for surgery. This is our best hospital. I called for a second ambulance and let the ship captain go in the first to Haiphong Hospital."

"The ship captain?" I asked, glancing over to Ti-Anna.

"At least, that's who we think he is," the inspector said. "An injured older gentleman who washed up on shore."

So I wasn't a murderer after all.

"As we reconstruct the events of the night, we believe he must have been carelessly smoking on deck, just before they were to set out," the inspector continued.

She gave me a look, I thought, or maybe I imagined it. I didn't say anything.

"It seems he will survive, but due to his injuries, we have not yet been able to speak with him. Also, a couple of the ringleaders may have escaped in the confusion," the inspector was saying. "Which is why we could use your help."

Leaving out only the small detail of the gasoline canister, I described what I had seen and heard as best I could, including the ship's name and Filipino flag, the odd language I had heard through the window, the men I'd seen on the wharf after the explosion.

The inspector barked some orders to someone outside my room, and a few minutes later a policeman came in and began speaking to me in a language I couldn't understand.

"Was this what you heard?"

I said I didn't think so. "Not Filipino," she said to herself. She dismissed the policeman and called for someone else. After a while a man in civilian clothes came in and spoke to me, equally unintelligibly.

"That sounds more like it," I said.

"Thai," she pronounced. "The girls were probably destined for Bangkok. No wonder they needed so much fuel."

She spoke quietly with her Thai-speaking deputy for a few minutes and then returned to me.

"Mr. Wynkoop, you have been most helpful," she said.

An orderly came in with what I guessed was meant to be lunch but looked like some glop you wouldn't serve your dog. Sydney saw my face and burst out laughing.

"I'm sure they thought they should cook you something Western," she said and, turning to the inspector, explained, "Ethan has become a fan of Hanoi-style pho."

The inspector, taking charge yet again, barked some orders to the orderly, who whisked the offending tray away.

"Enjoy your pho," she said as she adjusted her Cowboys hat. "Thank you again for your heroism. In the future, please be careful with fire on windy days."

And with that, Inspector Tranh was out the door.

Chapter 35

"Now," Ti-Anna said briskly. "Want to hear what else you've been missing?"

It wasn't really a question, so I didn't bother to reply.

Sydney had met our ambulance at the emergency room, Ti-Anna recounted, and the two of them had waited until I came out of surgery and they knew I was going to be okay. Then Ti-Anna had persuaded Sydney to go with her back to the house she'd been kidnapped from. The police had been through it by then, but they hadn't paid any attention to—

"The photographs," I said.

Ti-Anna nodded. She stood and walked over to the window. The girl with the doll followed with her eyes. I knew Ti-Anna was thinking again of the expression on her father's face.

"They're high quality," she said. "You could easily identify the Chinese agents. You can even read the license plate on one of the cars. Mr. Ky said it's from Kunming, in southwest China. Not that far from the border."

"Mr. Ky?"

"From the Vietnamese secret service or something. They're going to let us do a press conference tomorrow morning," Ti-Anna said. "You've got to get yourself cleaned up by then, okay?"

I wasn't sure what she meant by that, but just then the pho arrived.

"You're going to be fine, by the way, though it was a bad break— more than one, actually," she said. "That's a temporary cast. In a few days you'll need to have a different one put on."

I closed my eyes and imagined crossing a Hanoi street on crutches. I thought about trying to explain this cast to my mother. I thought about the giant spool, and how lucky I was that it hadn't landed a little higher up.

On the other hand, it would have been even luckier if it hadn't landed on me at all.

I ate my noodles and slept for a while. When I woke up Ti-Anna and the little girl were gone, having left a polo shirt and pair of sweatpants they must have bought for me.

I decided to see if I could get the hang of the crutches. Pretty soon I was swinging the length of the corridor, much to the dismay of the nurses, who seemed to think I should be in bed for another week or two. After a while my armpits hurt enough to take my mind off my other bumps and scrapes.

Day Seven: Saturday

Hanoi

Chapter 36

The next morning I practiced some more, slept some more, practiced, dozed, practiced.

Sydney, Ti-Anna and the girl with the doll showed up after lunch. They helped me downstairs and out the door, where a black government car was waiting. The driver dropped my crutches into the trunk as I settled in the front seat and swung my leg in. The girl with the doll sat in back, between Sydney and Ti-Anna.

"Would somebody explain what's happening?" I asked, when we were on the road.

Sydney laid out the plan: we would go public with evidence that Chinese agents had lured one of their country's most famous exiles into a trap in Vietnam, and then kidnapped him and driven him (we supposed) across the border and into a prison in the provincial capital of Kunming. People would be so outraged that the Chinese government would have to admit that they had him in custody.

"And let him go?" I asked

"Well . . ." Sydney hesitated. "Ideally, of course. But if not that, or not right away, at least admit they have him. Maybe eventually they'd allow him to have visitors, and announce the charges against him. Which would be a big improvement from having no idea where he is at all."

"Or whether," Ti-Anna said.

That was a conversation-stopper.

Sitting in the front of a car driving down a crowded Hanoi street turned out to be almost as terrifying as being one of the pedestrians dodging it. My theory that drivers were judiciously measuring the steady pace of pedestrians crossing in front of them? From this angle I wasn't so sure. Our driver honked and drove and honked some more, and apparently assumed that everyone would get out of his way. Which I guess they did, most of the time.

"Meanwhile, you might wonder why the Vietnamese government is letting you do this," Sydney suggested, which made me feel stupid, because I hadn't wondered at all.

"To thank us for helping to catch the traffickers?" I guessed.

When I'd checked out of the hospital, they had told me the government was graciously picking up the bill, because I had performed a service to law and order and to the unshakeable bonds of friendship between their people and our people, and so forth and so on.

"Well, that might be part of it," Sydney said, in a tone that suggested that in fact it had nothing to do with it whatsoever. "More likely, they're furious that Chinese agents would pull a stunt like this on their territory. They won't say anything publicly—and they won't be on the podium with you guys—but just letting this happen will show the Chinese how they feel."

"Us guys?" I asked. What were they expecting me to do?

"Us guys?" Ti-Anna asked, with a slight quaver. "Aren't you going to be with us?"

"You'll do fine," Sydney said.

And we did. Or rather, Ti-Anna did, because she did most of the talking, sometimes in English, sometimes in Chinese, depending on who was asking the questions.

There were a lot of TV cameras, and a lot of reporters, mostly Vietnamese, but not only. The BBC was there, and the Associated Press, and some Hong Kong networks, and even a crew affiliated with CNN.

Ti-Anna explained how the Chinese agents had set a trap, and why her father might have fallen for it—that he believed so passionately that his countrymen deserved to live in freedom, and was so dedicated to democracy in China, that he would have jumped at any chance to cooperate with people inside the country who felt the same way, even if maybe common sense was telling him to be careful.

She showed the photos, which some officials had helpfully enlarged to poster size. And then she explained how we'd fallen into the same trap, and how she'd been told that her disappearance would serve as a warning to anyone else who wanted to challenge the Chinese government, and how she'd been drugged and driven away.

I explained how I'd followed her on the roof of her truck, and what I'd found inside it when we finally got to the harbor. I described what happened to the ship the girls were meant to travel on.

Mostly the reporters were interested in Ti-Anna. And she was amazing—calm, clear, even eloquent.

"Your father would be proud," I whispered when it was over and we were just sitting up there, waiting for the TV lights to be switched off and for someone to unclip the little microphones from our shirts.

She smiled, and seemed to know I was right. The girl with the doll, who'd been reluctantly standing off to the side with Sydney, came running onto the podium to reclaim Ti-Anna's hand.

I thought that from here on in we could coast home, and that the scariest thing awaiting me now would be my parents.

Once again, I thought wrong.

Chapter 37

We celebrated, if you can call it that, with one more pho dinner. Without even asking, Sydney ordered me an extra bowl.

When we'd finished eating, she turned stern.

"This has gone on long enough," she said. "It's morning in Washington, and it's time for you both to call your parents. You two have done something heroic, but honestly you're also way over the line."

I couldn't argue. As focused on their Geneva conference as I hoped they were, my parents weren't likely to stay oblivious to our Hanoi press conference for long.

I wasn't looking forward to the call. I hadn't given my parents all that much thought over the past few days, terrible as that might sound. Everything had rushed at us so fast. And now there was so much to explain and apologize for—where would I even begin?

Sydney wasn't asking, though, she was telling. We followed her into her clanking elevator and up to the fourth floor. She sent Ti-Anna and the little girl into one office and me into another.

"I'll wait in my office," she said, after explaining how to make an international call. "Take your time."

While I was building up my courage, I signed on and found a series of emails—first from my brother, then my parents, my brother, my parents—each one more agitated than the one before.

"You know what?" I told myself. "This is going to be a lot easier to explain in person." Which I'd be able to do, in only a day or two. I could reassure them by email that I was all right.

I wrote that I'd be home soon and assured them that I was safe. `I'm really, really sorry to have made you worry` I typed. I hit Send.

There, I thought. That wasn't so hard. I hoped Sydney wouldn't ask any questions.

Ti-Anna and the girl with the rag doll were on the couch in Sydney's office when I walked in. Ti-Anna looked ashen, and not in a mood to discuss why.

"Did you make contact?" Sydney asked.

I nodded: one more technically true lie. She turned off the lights, locked up and led us to her apartment.

The three of us—Ti-Anna, the girl with the doll and I—spent the night on mattresses on Sydney's living room floor. She wasn't going to let us out of her sight again as long as we were in Vietnam, she said.

Day Eight: Sunday

Hanoi and Hong Kong

Chapter 38

In the morning we headed to the airport.

Amazingly, Sydney's colleague in the capital of Laos, Vientiane, had found a relative of the girl with the doll—an aunt, I think—and the organization had paid for her to fly to Hanoi in time to meet us before we boarded. The aunt was a thin woman with a tight black bun who didn't look all that much older than the girl. She crouched low and held open her arms when she saw her niece.

The girl looked at her without surprise or any other expression, dropped Ti-Anna's hand and walked to her aunt. But as they turned to leave, the girl whispered something in her aunt's ear and the aunt nodded. Then the girl walked back and held out her doll to Ti-Anna.

Ti-Anna looked questioningly at Sydney, who nodded too, so Ti-Anna took the doll and held the girl's hand once more.

We thanked Sydney and hugged her and promised to be in touch as soon as we landed in Hong Kong, where someone from the U.S. consulate would be meeting us so that—as Sydney said—we absolutely could not get into any more trouble before our flight the next day to Washington.

We boarded. We took off. And Ti-Anna seemed to deflate before my eyes.

At first I didn't notice. We were sitting in business class, courtesy of the Socialist Republic of Vietnam, which I thought was pretty exciting, and I was studying the Vietnam Air menu for the short flight to Hong Kong.

But by the time we reached twenty-five thousand feet (or eight thousand meters, as the pilot said), I realized she'd barely spoken since we boarded.

"What's wrong?" I asked.

For the longest time she didn't answer. She had the window seat, and she stared out at the layer of clouds beneath us. She was still clutching the little girl's rag doll, which made her seem even more forlorn.

"You know those good-news, bad-news jokes?" she finally said, still staring out the window, and speaking so softly I could barely hear her over the engines. "That's what it felt like last night when my mother answered the phone, so hopeful and pathetic. Good news: your husband is alive. Bad news: he's back in a Chinese prison and may never come home."

She turned and looked at me with empty eyes. "She didn't get the joke."

I hadn't seen her like this since—well, since that day behind school when she had told me that her father was missing. Which felt like a million years ago.

"I think my mother had convinced herself that my father was going to walk back in the apartment at any moment," she said. "And now, she's getting just me. Empty-handed."

She looked down at the rag doll in her lap, as if mystified at how it had gotten there.

"You're not empty-handed," I insisted. "First of all, you rescued a hundred Laotian peasant girls from slavery. Doesn't that count for something?"

No response.

"And as for your father—if it weren't for you, we'd have no idea whether he was alive or dead, and we might never have heard a word from the Chinese government. Ever. Now they'll have to admit the truth—and then, before you know it, they'll have to let him go."

That last part sounded stupid even to me, and as soon as I said it I wished I had quit half a sentence sooner. Ti-Anna just looked at me, but without seeing me, and turned back to the window.

"I don't know how I can go back to my mother empty-handed," I barely heard her say. She wasn't talking to me anymore, but to the clouds. Or to herself.

I didn't know what else to say, and after a while I dozed off. When I awoke, the jet was descending. Ti-Anna still was staring out the window.

Chapter 39

It shouldn't have surprised me that our Hanoi news conference would be big news in Hong Kong, but I wasn't prepared for the crush of cameras and reporters waiting beyond customs.

We pushed through, saying nothing as the reporters yelled at us, mostly in Chinese. Ti-Anna, unsmiling, acted as if she didn't even see them.

"Ethan? Ti-Anna?"

A booming voice separated itself from the clamor. A big guy was planted just beyond the cameras. Buzz cut, polo shirt, ID on a lanyard around his neck.

"Brian Bates, U.S. consulate." He held out his hand. I shook it, but saw out of the corner of my eye that Ti-Anna was looking dubious.

Brian saw too.

He held his ID out for our inspection. "Sydney said I should promise you—" He stopped and dug a crumpled Post-it out of his pocket. "Pho bo? Does that sound right?"

Despite herself, Ti-Anna smiled fleetingly. We fell in with Brian.

He had a friendly but commanding presence, and between that and Ti-Anna's forbidding expression—and maybe the risk of getting too near one of my crutches—the reporters fell away.

"I have instructions to keep you safe for the next"—he looked at his watch—"nineteen hours."

He gestured toward our day packs. "That's all you've got?" We nodded. "Impressive. C'mon, then. I've got a car waiting."

Just before the sliding doors, Ti-Anna excused herself to use the ladies' room. Brian started to follow her, then checked himself but watched until she'd disappeared into the bathroom.

We stood silently for a moment or two. It was awkward.

"Thanks for doing this," I said. "You must have a lot more important work you could be doing."

"Are you kidding?" he answered. He didn't look at me; his gaze was fixed on the ladies' room door. His tone was amiable, though. "Ordinarily I have three jobs: handing out visas, refusing visas and taking complaints from people in the second category. Getting out of the office is a holiday for me."

Outside there was another official black car with another official driver, who helped tuck in my leg, this time into the backseat, and dropped my crutches in the trunk. I could get used to this, I thought.

We started along the incredible bridges and causeways that connect the airport to the city. It didn't make sense, I knew—after all, we were a lot closer to China now than we had been in Hanoi—but somehow I felt safer, almost as if this were a homecoming.

Which, in a funny way, made me think about the real homecoming that lay ahead. Where would be the first place I'd go when I got home? I wondered. The bagel store, probably. Order whatever kind was hottest. Poppy seed, with luck.

I turned to say something dumb about bagels to Ti-Anna, but the look on her face froze me. She was staring out her window, but not seeing the bay. If anything, she looked grimmer than she had on the plane.

Brian twisted toward us from the front seat. "Let's discuss where you guys are going to stay," he said.

Ti-Anna didn't reply.

"We have a hotel room," I told him.

I didn't want to see that place, or its mountainous desk clerk, ever again. But I also didn't want to go home without my brother's backpack.

"Let's go pick up your things, and then you can stay with me," Brian said. "I've got a futon and a pullout couch, nice hot shower, satellite TV. Even the view's not bad. How does that sound?"

Ti-Anna remained silent.

I said, "Are you sure? We hate to impose on you." It sounded pretty nice. Not to mention free.

We drove up Nathan Road to the entrance to our hotel. Brian said a few words to the driver, and the three of us went in—along the same dingy shopping alley, squeezing into the same airless elevator.

The scary desk clerk eyed us without surprise and began demanding money. Brian cut him short, rattling along in impressive-sounding Chinese as he gestured toward the elevator, and down the corridor, and even behind the fat man's desk. The man looked at Brian with loathing, but fell silent.

Brian waited outside Room 23 while I stuffed my belongings into my brother's backpack and Ti-Anna picked up her duffel.

"What did he say to the guy?" I whispered.

"He was reciting all the building code violations he had noticed, and the fire code violations, and what the fine for each one is," Ti-Anna whispered back, with a touch of admiration. "He seemed to know what he was talking about."

"Okay," Brian said as I happily left Room 23 for the last time. "Let's go."

Unexpectedly, Ti-Anna broke in.

"How about one last Hong Kong meal?" she said. "We can show you an amazing noodle place not far from here."

I looked at her, stunned. Had just reclaiming her bag lifted her out of her funk? Or was it realizing we'd never have to see the Rising Phoenix again? Brian looked dubious too—like he'd be a lot happier getting us safely into his condo and feeding us instant ramen.

But Ti-Anna said, "Our treat," and gave him one of her trademark smiles.

Brian shrugged, as if to say, what harm can there be.

"I doubt there's a noodle place in Kowloon that you can show me," he said. "But go ahead, bring it on."

Which I guess you could say she did.

Chapter 40

She waited until we'd been served to make her move.

As soon as she got up to use the bathroom, I should have known. I'd been traveling with her long enough to know that not only was I always hungry before her, but I always needed a bathroom first too—she was a camel.

I was so happy with the bowl in front of me that I didn't give it a thought, which was undoubtedly what Ti-Anna—having traveled with me for a while—had counted on. Brian seemed pretty focused on his soup noodles with shredded pork and pickled vegetables. He watched Ti-Anna disappear into the back of the restaurant, but he didn't stop slurping.

So she got a pretty good head start. I don't know how many minutes passed before it occurred to me that too many minutes had passed. Three? Four? Maybe even five?

When I said something to Brian, he froze, chopsticks midway between bowl and mouth. Then the chopsticks fell into his soup with a little splash as he leapt to his feet.

"Don't move," he said to me. "Do not move."

A few customers looked up, startled, as he ran to the back. I imagine he pushed into the ladies' room, and when that was empty, tried the kitchen, and then the men's room. He was back in seconds, cursing so vociferously that even in the middle of everything I was impressed.

"I am so screwed," he said, when he was finally able to complete a sentence. Except he didn't say "screwed." I remember thinking, So Ti-Anna's been kidnapped and what comes to mind is that *you're* screwed?

After a few more strings of curses, he got himself under control.

"Okay," he said. "I'm going to call for help, and then I'm going to go look for her. You stay here. Do not move. Got that?" I nodded. "I'll arrange for some police to get here and keep an eye on you. But it's probably just her they were after, right? You should be okay. Here. In case you need me."

He scribbled his cell phone number and was out the front door, punching in a call as he left.

As soon as he was out of sight, I swung my way to the back of the restaurant. By this time the owner was yelling with almost as much spirit as Brian. Probably about the bill, I supposed, but I didn't stay to find out.

The kitchen was narrow and sweltering, and one crutch nearly slid out from under me on the slick floor. A crate of bok choy propped open the back door, which gave onto a narrow alley, dark, amazingly cool in contrast . . .

. . . and empty. No sign of her, of course.

Left? Right? I chose left, for no reason, and followed the alley to the nearest main street, where the usual crowds were streaming by. There was no hope of tracking her, that was for sure. A five-minute head start in this city, when you had no clue where to start, was as good as five hours, whether she was on her own or she'd been kidnapped.

I didn't believe she'd been kidnapped. I wasn't going to tell Brian, but in my gut I *knew* she hadn't been kidnapped. She'd come to some decision on the plane from Hanoi, or maybe in the car, when she was staring at the bay so unseeingly, and so unhappy.

How can I go back to my mother empty-handed? she'd said. What did that mean? I couldn't believe she would, well, do anything to harm herself. Surely she'd know that would make things a thousand times worse for her mother.

I also knew people could do crazy things when they worked themselves into a state like Ti-Anna had.

Of course it hurt that she had kept whatever she was planning secret not just from Brian but from me, too. But I wasn't going to worry about that now. I was going to find her.

I found myself limping toward the bay as I tried to puzzle things out. Before I realized it, I was at the harbor, on the walkway we'd come to that first night. The lights were coming on, the ferries were zipping back and forth, couples were strolling and holding hands and talking on their phones. None of it looked beautiful or exciting anymore.

I took my phone out of my knapsack for the first time in days. I thought, if there's anyone she might trust here, it would be Horace. He had sent us to Radio Man, but I didn't think Horace had been in on any of this, and I knew Ti-Anna didn't think so either.

Before I could try to track him down, I noticed that a call had been made from my phone at 4:38 a.m.

Chapter 41

It made no sense to me.

At 4:38 we'd been fast asleep on Sydney's floor. Could the girl with the doll have played with my phone while I slept? It didn't seem likely.

Then I remembered: I'd set the phone to stay on Bethesda time. On Hong Kong time, the call would have gone out at 3:38 p.m., not 4:38 a.m. Around the time we had landed in Hong Kong.

Or rather, I realized, at exactly the time Ti-Anna had told Brian she needed to use the airport ladies' room.

Concentrate, I instructed myself. She must have taken the phone while I was sleeping on the plane. Carried it off, made a call from the bathroom and then stuck it back in my bag during the ride from the airport, or in the coffin elevator, or somewhere else along the way.

Whom had she called?

The number was local. When I hit redial, a girl answered right away.

"Hello?" she said. "Ti-Anna?"

"This is Ethan," I said slowly. And I then knew who was on the other end: Wei, who we'd met near this very spot. The bubbly one, who looked like Ti-Anna.

"Hi!" she said. "What a trip you had! Of course Mai and I saw you on TV, and we were so excited! And then Ti-Anna told me all about how brave you were!"

"I was?" I said. "I mean, she did?"

"Yes, of course!" Wei burbled. "But she'd probably be mad at me for telling you so!" She giggled.

"Oh, I don't think she'd mind," I said, stalling for time. What was going on?

There was a tiny pause.

"Is something wrong?" Wei asked. "Why are you calling? Did the reporters find you?"

The reporters? "Um, no," I said. "I was just wondering if Ti-Anna was still with you."

"No, I left her a few minutes ago! I thought you were going to meet at the Y."

The Y? I wasn't getting any less confused. Whatever Ti-Anna was up to, it wasn't what Wei thought she was up to, and I didn't want to make her suspicious.

"No," I said. "I think I must have gotten the time wrong, or something, that's why I was calling. What exactly did she say again?" I asked.

"Well, that you two were going to stay at the Y tonight, before flying home, but if she checked in with her real name, the reporters would track you down, so I lent her my ID," Wei said, her voice bubbling again at the idea of playing a part in this adventure.

"You *what?*" I said, before I could stop myself. "I mean, did she say how she was going to get it back to you?"

"Yes, she said she'd leave it in an envelope at the desk of the Y,"

Wei said. "My parents would probably kill me, but I think she is so brave. Like you! I was happy to help!"

"That is so nice," I said. "Did she take anything else?" Why would Ti-Anna want Wei's Hong Kong ID?

"No," Wei said. "Actually, I keep my Home Return Card in the same billfold, and I just gave her the whole thing."

My heart sank. Her Home Return Card—I knew from the guide-book that that was what China gave Hong Kong residents who wanted to travel to the mainland. A China visa, in other words. Except since it was all one country, they couldn't call it a visa.

"Why?" Wei asked. The note of doubt was back, a bit stronger this time. "Is something wrong?"

"No, no, I just . . . I just wondered if maybe I'm in the wrong place, or something. Are there two Y's?"

I was babbling now, trying not to alarm Wei while my mind raced to imagine what Ti-Anna might be up to. One thing was for sure, she wasn't planning to give Wei her document back in the morning. And she must be awfully desperate to involve this sweet girl.

"Not really," Wei said. "At least, when anyone says the Y, they mean the main one. On the Kowloon side?"

"That's what I figured," I said. "Well, I'm sure I screwed up some-how. There wouldn't be anything unusual about that."

I paused. "What else did you guys talk about? I'm sorry I didn't get a chance to see you."

"We didn't have much time," Wei said. "I promised my parents I'd be home before dark. She told me a little about what happened to you in Vietnam, like I said. I told her how we were going up to the beach on Hainan Island next week. She asked me what it's like, and how we get there—she talked about how, even with her father and everything, she'd like to go back into China someday."

"'How you get there'?" I repeated. Hainan was a resort inside China proper. "What do you mean?"

"You know, do we fly, or take the train, or whatever," she answered. "She asked about Lo Wu, where we cross into the mainland, and how that works, whether pedestrians can cross. But we take the train. We talked about school a little. And how neither one of us is looking forward to it! And she promised to come visit again. You better come too!"

"Definitely!" I said. "Or you to Washington."

"I wish!" Wei said. "All right, I'd better go. Friend me as soon as you get home, all right?"

"Definitely," I said again. "Thanks, Wei."

My heart had sunk even lower. Ti-Anna didn't intend to be in Bethesda two days from now, friending Wei or anyone else. I realized that she didn't plan on being on a plane to Dulles tomorrow. I wasn't going to get on that plane without her, though. I knew that now.

Ti-Anna was heading into China with Wei's ID and Home Return Card. Somehow she thought she was going to rescue her father from prison in Kunming.

What she really was going to do was get herself locked up. For a long, long time.

Chapter 42

My guidebook was in my pack—in the trunk of Brian's car. I stumped as fast as I could to the nearest fancy hotel, the Regent, found its gift shop and pulled a guidebook from the rotating shelf.

Speed-scanning, I learned I could get to Lo Wu via the Kowloon–Canton Railway, which left from the Hung Hom station, which was just a few blocks away. I shoved the book back and swung my way there. The train accepted the same Octopus card as the subway and the ferry. I boarded as the doors were closing. Trains left every five or ten minutes, I saw, so Ti-Anna might have a pretty good lead on me. How good, I didn't know.

It was a forty-minute ride through the darkness, which gave me time to think, but I wouldn't say I was thinking clearly. Mostly I tried to imagine what Ti-Anna thought she was up to.

Somehow she might get to Kunming, I could believe that. She looked enough like Wei to travel on her ID, and her Chinese was good enough not to make anyone suspicious.

Somehow, though I had no idea how, she might even find the

191

prison where they were holding her dad—if he had in fact been taken to Kunming, and if he hadn't been moved since.

Then what? She thought she could make *them* see reason? Or she'd smuggle him a file inside a moon cake?

Eventually Wei would report her card as lost or stolen. Would she tell who had stolen it? Maybe not. She might still feel loyal to Ti-Anna, even when her card wasn't at the Y tomorrow morning. Or she might feel embarrassed to have been duped.

All in all, Ti-Anna might figure she'd have a few days inside China before *they* even knew she was there.

What I knew for sure was that she had a way into China and I didn't, and so I had to stop her at the border.

As soon as I saw Lo Wu, I should have realized how impossible that would be.

Thousands of people go back and forth every day, so of course the border crossing was an enormous complex: barracks and buildings and fences and lines and intimidating signs everywhere.

There were a dozen lines in a glaringly bright terminal, and hundreds of people snaking back and forth, patiently waiting to present their documents. I raced from one line to the next: no Ti-Anna. I made myself do it again, slowly, face by face; maybe she'd disguised herself in some way.

Of course she wasn't there.

I couldn't wait inside the building. Either you were in line, or you had no reason to be there, and I didn't exactly blend in.

I sat by a scraggly bush out in the shadows, from where I could see inside the waiting hall. Crushed juice boxes and empty beer cans were scattered around me, and diesel fumes mixed with a faint odor of urine. I'd been starving. Now I felt nauseous.

And so I waited, feeling foolish.

At some level I must have known it was hopeless, even as I tried to examine each arriving person, the businessmen with their briefcases, the young moms with children and backpacks full of presents for the grandparents across the border.

Of course she wouldn't have disguised herself: the whole point was how much she resembled Wei. Maybe she hadn't come here at all. These days there were many ways to cross into China: trains, buses, even ferries that would take you to cities up and down the Pearl River Delta. For all I knew, she had asked Wei about this one to throw me off.

I couldn't admit that I had failed to stop her. And I couldn't think what else to do.

I didn't realize that I'd dozed off until I woke up, befuddled. The immigration hall was dark. In fact it must have been the quiet that woke me.

I stood stiffly and remembered why I was there. The darkness was like a final verdict of failure. I made my way back to the station.

Midnight had passed, and I had missed the last return train. The next wouldn't leave until five-something, I learned from a man still inside the ticket booth.

He was gray-haired, soft-spoken, and when I looked bereft (not to mention bedraggled, I'm sure) he seemed to take pity. He told me where I could still find a taxi to take me back to Kowloon.

It would cost a small fortune, but I was past caring. I was low on cash, though, so I asked the man where I could find an ATM, and he pointed me back across the station.

Standing before that ATM machine, in the nearly deserted Lo Wu railway station, was where I discovered that my Visa card was missing.

Day Nine: Monday

Hong Kong and Washington, D.C.

Chapter 43

The empty slot in my wallet shocked me into finally thinking straight.

I sprint-crutched my way back across the deserted station. The man in the booth looked a little exasperated when I reappeared.

"This is going to sound crazy," I said. He looked up at me, without expression. "I'm sure you want to get home. But could you possibly do me a giant favor? It's an emergency."

He waited patiently, if a bit warily.

"I need to know when was the last flight from Hong Kong to Kunming today, and when's the first flight tomorrow."

"Kunming? You mean in Yunnan province?"

I nodded. It's possible my pronunciation wasn't native quality.

He looked me over skeptically.

"And this is an emergency?"

I nodded.

He sighed, put on the bifocals that he kept hanging around his neck and turned to his computer. In a minute he came back to the microphone in the window.

"There are four flights a day," he said. "The last one today was at three-fifty p.m. The first one out tomorrow is Dragon Air Flight 2435 at nine-fifty-five a.m."

"Thank you!" I said, with so much feeling that the clerk looked alarmed for the first time.

She could not have flown out yet. I still had a chance.

"That's all you need?" he asked.

I nodded and tried to calm myself.

"Thank you," I said again. "You are very kind."

It wasn't all I needed, but there wasn't much the man in the booth could do about the rest of my problems. I didn't have enough money for a taxi back to Kowloon, let alone to the airport, and without my credit card obviously I couldn't get more. But if I caught the first train back, and then the airport bus, I should still have time.

In the darkest corner of the station I slid down with my back against a tiled wall and my broken leg straight out. I was sure Hong Kong police wouldn't look kindly on this kind of vagrancy, but a couple of men in uniform had strolled through while I'd been talking to the man in the booth, and I hoped it had been their last sweep of the night. The ticket man himself had deliberately looked the other way as I walked off, I thought. The booth was shuttered now.

I wondered where Ti-Anna was at that moment.

I thought I finally understood what she had done.

When she had called from Sydney's office, her mother's reaction must have been even more unbearable than Ti-Anna had let on. It had eaten at her until she decided she just couldn't return with the news that her father was, once again, in a Chinese prison, and that neither of them could do anything about it.

It made me angry. Somebody I loved—yes, on the gritty floor of a dark, deserted train station, I admitted that to myself—somebody I had done so much for had betrayed me. While I was fast asleep, she had lifted my phone from my backpack and my Visa card from my wallet. She hadn't trusted me enough to tell me her plans, and she had left me on my own and close to broke.

I felt sad—sad that she felt so desperate that she couldn't tell me what she was going to do.

By keeping it a secret she'd been trying to protect me, I understood that, and to make sure I wouldn't try to stop her. On some level she had to know that her plan was crazy enough that this time I wouldn't have tagged reluctantly behind. I would have done everything in my power to wrench her onto that jet to Washington.

I was still going to do that, if I could.

All I could do was lean against the wall and miss her—miss the real Ti-Anna, the one who had disappeared not from the noodle shop but somewhere high over the South China Sea.

I set my phone to buzz at five a.m. and closed my eyes.

Of course I couldn't sleep. I played and replayed how Ti-Anna had pulled this off, imagining slightly different details each time.

From the airport bathroom, she had arranged to meet Wei somewhere near the noodle restaurant, that much was sure. She had pulled off her surprise while we were eating, had run off and—for once not getting lost—found Wei. Then, after pocketing Wei's ID, she had used the Visa card, maybe at a few different machines, to get enough cash to buy a ticket to Kunming.

She would have wanted to fly straight there, and not waste time on buses or trains. I was sure of that now too. At nine-fifty a.m., traveling as Wang Wei, law-abiding Hong Kong high school student, she'd be sitting on Dragon Air Flight 2435. As for what she would do from there on in, I didn't have a clue. But maybe she did. At a minimum, I knew the set of her jaw would make it look like she did.

I was sure I was right this time about her plans. I wasn't at all sure how I would keep her from carrying them out.

I just knew I had to find her.

Chapter 44

I guess in the end I did doze off, because my stomach growled me awake before my phone had a chance to buzz. I think I'd been dreaming of that bowl of noodles I'd abandoned when Ti-Anna disappeared. I didn't dare use any of my scarce remaining money on food.

At first it seemed as though things would go my way. I boarded the first train with a few sleepy Monday-morning commuters. Back at the Hung Hom station I had to wait only five minutes before the airport express bus pulled in. A couple of other travelers stood aside for me and my crutches.

But when I pressed my Octopus card to the fare machine, it answered with an angry buzz, like I'd answered wrong in a quiz show.

"Need more money," the driver said in heavily accented English.

The fare was forty-five dollars (Hong Kong). I had thirteen dollars left on my card. I took what I had out of my wallet, and then dug into my pockets, trying to separate Hong Kong coins from Vietnamese dong while the others waiting to board began to shift and press impatiently.

"Pay or step away," the driver said.

"I don't have quite enough," I finally had to admit, and then held out my bills and coins. "Is there any way you could let me on with this? I really, really need to get to the airport."

"Everybody really, really need to go somewhere," the driver said. "Please step away."

Then, throwing me a crumb, he said, "City bus A33 much cheaper. Change at Tung Chung."

So I stumped off to find city bus A33, which was in fact much cheaper.

And much, much slower.

Everyone will tell you Hong Kong is a tiny place, and if you compare it to China of course that's true. But if you're driving to the airport through the jumble of Kowloon, instead of on those airy causeways, it doesn't seem all that tiny.

To me it seemed endless—block after block after congested block. My bus driver seemed to want to savor every storefront. He stopped at yellow lights. He slowed for green lights, as if hoping they would turn yellow. When they stayed green, there was always someone waiting to board at the corner, usually a bent-over old lady, and by the time she made it up the steps and finished fumbling through her purse, the light was red. Or yellow. Or about to turn yellow, which seemed enough to persuade the driver that he ought to wait a cycle.

I began to sweat.

The longer we drove, the worse the traffic seemed to get. I went forward to ask how long it would take, but the driver didn't speak English. I sat back down, staring at my watch, cursing every red light, and every elderly passenger, and most of all, my infuriating driver. I had had plenty of time. Now it was going to be close.

At the Tung Chung terminus it got worse. I couldn't find the airport shuttle, and the information line seemed frozen. I stood in it for a while, gave up to go looking for the bus, came back to find the line even longer.

When I finally boarded what I thought was the right bus, it sat for what seemed an eternity, before a driver showed up and finally got us moving.

By the time I reached the airport it was eight-forty a.m. I had figured I'd be at the Dragon Air counter by seven, which would have been plenty of time. Now as I hobbled to Dragon Air check-in, I was despairing. She'd probably spent the night in the airport—maybe on the same patch of floor we'd staked out before flying to Hanoi—and been the first to check in. Even seven might have been too late. Eight-forty was hopeless.

At the counter I had to wait in another line, of course, and when I reached the counter they wouldn't tell me if Wang Wei had checked in, or even if she was on the plane.

"You don't understand," I said. "I have to know."

I was nearly shouting, realizing even as I did that I was doing myself no good. I can only imagine how I looked and smelled, crazed, having spent part of the night in a beery bush and the rest on a train station floor.

Ti-Anna was a few hundred yards away, about to take a step that would ruin her life. And I couldn't even talk to her.

Then I had one last thought.

"Where's the United counter?" I asked.

Chapter 45

It was a distance. Everything was a distance in the Hong Kong airport. But when I got there I found no line whatsoever.

"You're here awfully early," the lone woman behind the counter said when I showed her my ticket to D.C. "Check-in won't start for four more hours."

"I promised my mother I'd go through security first thing in the morning, she's so worried I'll miss my plane," I said, in as earnest a voice as I could muster. "Is there any way you could check me in?"

She gave me a long look but eventually took my ticket.

"Let me see what I can do," she said.

She scanned my passport into her machine and then gave me an even longer look. Had Brian put me on some no-fly list? My heart was beating so hard I was sure she'd hear it.

"No luggage?" she asked. "And aren't you rather young to be taking such a long trip on your own?"

"I guess that's true," I said. Please, give me my boarding pass. There's no time for small talk. "A school trip. I stayed a little longer than the others, to finish my project. Sent most of my stuff back with them."

"Oh?" she said, as if she had all the time in the world. She was a middle-aged Chinese lady, more like a schoolteacher than an airline employee. "What did your project concern?"

"Urban ecology," I blurted. Now I had no idea what was going to come out of my mouth. "Wildlife in an urban setting. Especially snakes on Lamma Island."

"How unusual," she murmured, as her machine spit out my boarding pass. Please don't be a herpetologist, I thought.

Mercifully another traveler had lined up behind me. "Seat thirty-six F," she said as she handed me my pass. Apparently my name had set off no alarm bells. "This is your gate number, but there's no point in going there before noon. Security is right that way."

By the time I got through and raced to the Kunming flight, everyone had boarded. One young gate agent was tidying up behind the counter.

The door, I saw, was still open. I still had a chance.

"I need a word with someone who is on the plane," I told him.

Once again I gave no thought to the impression I must have made, swaying on my crutches, sweat pouring down. And no doubt sounding as though my life depended on his saying yes. Which is how I felt.

"Sir, are you on this flight?" he asked.

"No, but my—" I was going to say sister but realized he might not swallow that one. "My friend is, and I have some family news she needs to hear before she leaves."

"I can't let you on, sir," he said.

"Can you get her?" I said. "Please. It is so urgent, you have to believe me."

He looked me over.

"If you give me a note, I will take it to her," he said. "What is her name?"

"Wang Wei," I said. "Do you have a piece of paper I could borrow?"

He pushed a sheet of paper across the counter while he looked over the manifest.

"Yes, she's on board," he said.

I wasn't even relieved to hear it. I had known she would be.

"You'll have to be quick. We'll be closing the doors in a couple of minutes."

I stood with my pen in the air, afraid to begin. This would be the most important thing I had ever written, and I had no idea what to say.

If I had time, I thought, I could convince her. I could make her understand how crazy she was to be flying off to China alone, how wrong she was to feel like she'd failed on this trip, how terrible her father would feel if she went in after him. How happy her mother would be to have her back—even, as she put it, empty-handed.

How happy I would be.

But I didn't have time to explain it all. I didn't even have time to think. So I just started writing.

Dear Ti-Anna, I wrote. *If something is wrong in the world, it's wrong not to try to fix it. But if you have friends who want to help, it's wrong not to let them.*

And Ti-Anna, you have friends who want to help. Think of Sydney. And Horace. Think of Wei, so happy to play a part. The girl with the doll, who needed you. Even Radio Man, running out to us on the rocks. He did a bad thing, but he saved our lives too.

And think of me. We can do this together. If he isn't home by Christmas, we'll go in together. Next summer. I promise.

"Time is running out," the man said.

I scribbled, *Your friend, Ethan,* and handed the note to him, and he disappeared out the gangway with it.

The next minutes were the longest of my life, and when I saw the man coming back, alone, I thought it was all over.

But then she was there, walking a few steps behind him, my note in one hand, her duffel in the other, tears rolling down her face.

She didn't say anything, just dropped her stuff and put her arms around me. We held each other. Nothing had ever felt as good.

"Miss?" the agent said, not unkindly. "Will you be flying to Kunming, or will you not?"

She shook her head.

"Can she get her money back?" I asked over her shoulder. Ti-Anna choked out something between a sob and a laugh.

"I'm afraid not," he said. "She can get a Dragon Air credit, good for one year."

"Even better," I said. "We might be needing that."

Chapter 46

She clung to me while the attendant locked the gangway door. She held on while he collected his boarding pass stubs and switched off the announcement board behind him. We were still together when he walked away.

Finally, she let go, but not of my hand. We sat beside each other on the floor of the empty lounge, amid abandoned newspapers and half-filled coffee cups. She closed her eyes and folded her legs beneath her, lotus-style. Tears still rolled down her cheeks. She seemed not to notice.

I tried to imagine everything roiling through her. Exhaustion and hunger, for starters; I doubted she had eaten or slept since giving us the slip.

Relief, I hoped, that she had been saved from herself.

Defeat, no question, because this was the end to any fantasy that we'd be bringing her father home.

Dread, at how her mother would react.

And, maybe, I thought, a little gladness, at seeing me.

When she finally opened her eyes, she said, "Ethan, you know

I—I didn't want to lie to you. I knew you wouldn't let me go. I thought—" She stopped.

"I know," I said. "At least, I think I know." I paused. "We'll have time to talk about it."

"Yes," she said. "In the meantime—thank you."

We found a place for breakfast and ordered two giant bowls of noodles with dumplings on the side. You had to pay first. Sheepishly, she handed me the credit card.

Then I called Brian.

"The good news is I've found Ti-Anna, and she's fine, and we're both already at the airport," I said.

"Thank God," he breathed. And then, as though he really would have preferred to end the conversation right there, "What's the bad news?"

"We're through security, but she hasn't checked in," I said.

"That's impossible," Brian said.

"But true," I said. "Do you think you could help us out, one last time?"

"I can be there in an hour," he said. *"Do not move."* And then: "I mean it this time."

This time we did too. We finished our breakfast and ordered cups of tea, and sat, and talked a little, and sat some more.

"So how bad was it when you called your parents?" Ti-Anna asked.

I told her that I had not, technically speaking, called my parents. She gave me a look, but then stared into her cup.

"I guess I'm in no position to lecture about being honest with the people you love," she said.

I let that wash over me.

Then I asked, "Were you trying to throw me off when you asked Wei about crossing by land?"

Ti-Anna shook her head. "I was just trying to make sure there wasn't a smarter way in," she said. "And save you some money. But it seemed way too complicated."

I nodded. "Once I thought about it, I knew you'd fly. And I figured you'd prefer the sound of 'Dragon Air' to 'East China Air Lines.'"

"It did seem like a good omen that Dragon Air had the first flight out," she said.

Ti-Anna found a piece of paper and worked on a note to Wei. An hour after I'd called, Brian showed up.

He sat down at our table and asked where we'd been all night, but when I said it might make his life simpler if he didn't know, he agreed to go along with that. He took Ti-Anna's passport and my boarding pass and disappeared for a while, and when he returned he had a boarding pass for her and checked-luggage tags for each of us. My brother would get his backpack after all.

"I'm very sorry for the trouble I caused you," Ti-Anna said.

He waved her apology away with his big hand.

"To tell you the truth," he said, "everyone in the consulate admires the heck out of what you both did down there. But we were worried sick, as you can imagine."

"The heck"? I thought. You can do better than that, I happen to know.

"Actually, I have one more favor to ask." Ti-Anna handed him Wei's ID, with her note, and Brian promised to deliver them. When we started to say our good-byes, he interrupted us.

"I'm instructed to stick around until you are actually on the plane," he said. "Probably until you're in international air space, in fact." Then he added hastily: "Not that I don't trust you, of course."

"Of course," I said. "The noodles here aren't bad."

Brian ordered a large bowl, pulled up a chair and entertained us with tales from Mongolia, where he'd been posted before coming to Hong Kong. As we boarded, he shook our hands and assured us there were no hard feelings.

"One piece of advice, though," he said. "I'm only a grunt in the consulate, but I do hear things. And what I hear is, the Chinese aren't happy with you two. You might want to assume that you've got company on every phone call, and an extra reader on any email you send. They know how to do it."

That gave us something to think about on the long flight home.

Chapter 47

The flight home was our last chance to be together without parents and rules and other interference.

We were exhausted, though, and I don't think either of us was picturing what lay ahead.

I had just spent the most intense nine days with Ti-Anna that I'd ever spent with anyone. I'd also just spent the most intense twelve hours apart from Ti-Anna that I'd ever spent apart from anyone. It felt as though it would take both of us a while to work our way back from that.

We slept a lot, and not always at the same time. She started watching a movie in Chinese but fell asleep about five minutes in. I slipped off her earphones and tucked a blanket around her.

That was when the Chinese student came by.

The attendants had taken away the dinner trays and turned down the lights so people could sleep. The woman next to me got up to use the bathroom—Ti-Anna and I were in the middle two seats of a four-seat row—and a young man slipped into the empty seat, like he'd been waiting for a chance.

"I saw you on TV," he whispered. "You and your friend."

"Oh?" I said warily.

"I just want you to know," he whispered. "Not all Chinese people agree with what our government is doing."

"You're from China?"

"Shanghai," he said. "On my way to university in America."

"Oh?" I asked again, a little less warily. "Which one?"

The seat's rightful occupant returned.

"Doesn't matter," the student said. "Just tell her"—he pointed to Ti-Anna, a lump under her thin airline blanket—"some of us think her father is right. And brave." And he went back to his seat.

At Dulles, as the plane taxied to the gate, Ti-Anna took my hand one more time, and we sat quietly for one more minute.

We were back in America.

Chapter 48

Passport control, luggage, customs, it all went smoothly. We walked through the automatic doors into a crowd that almost made me nostalgic for Hanoi. Families were yelling for their Hong Kong relatives, professional drivers waved cards with the names of businesspeople they were supposed to meet, porters with luggage carts tried to drum up business.

At first I didn't see anyone I knew.

Then I saw him leaning in a relaxed way against a pillar across the concourse: blue suit, tight haircut. I recalled Brian's warning.

I poked Ti-Anna.

"Look who came to meet us," I said.

Her eyes narrowed. Then we both saw something else, a frantic movement at the far edge of the crowd.

I have to admit, my first thought was, I wonder whose busy schedule made my parents late this time, Mom's or Dad's?

In my defense, my next thought was only a millisecond away: you've got a lot of gall even *thinking* about complaining about your parents—about anything, anywhere, ever again.

Then I didn't have any thoughts at all, just relief and love and gratitude gushing through me. There was my mom in front, looking totally mom-ish as she firmly but politely pushed her way toward us. And—I had to do a double-take, or maybe it was a triple—there was Ti-Anna's mom, holding hands with mine. My dad and brother and sister were right behind.

Don't get the wrong idea: My parents were furious. Steaming, even. Incensed. Enraged. Not One Bit Amused. In fact, it would take me days to find out how angry they really were.

But they were also totally happy, and the happy part came before the mad part. I thought they might never let me go, and that felt great, but when we did finally stop hugging, I saw that Ti-Anna's mother still had her arms around Ti-Anna, eyes closed, head on her chest. If my mother hadn't gently patted her shoulder, the two of them might still be in the terminal.

Even though my parents had never met Ti-Anna, they hugged her, too, and so did my sister. Her mother shook my hand in a friendly way and said something in Chinese, as if a few days in Hong Kong ought to have been plenty for me to master the language. My brother pretended to inspect his backpack with an eye toward charging me for any damage, and we moved in one tight, noisy pack toward our van.

It felt good to be home.

As far as my summer went, things pretty much went downhill from there.

June–July.

Washington, D.C.

Chapter 49

I had to hand over the credit card, and my phone, which hurt worse. I didn't argue. My mother had some choice words as she showed me how much we'd spent.

I found a job. It's in an ice cream place in Bethesda. It's not bad, really. I started work on my third day back. The other kids working there are nice. At the rate I'm earning, I figure I'll be able to pay back what I owe in, oh, twenty-seven years.

As I say, that was the third day. On my second day back, we had to visit the police.

My parents had turned out not to be quite as clueless as I had counted on. Days before they got my email from Hanoi, they had figured out that I wasn't visiting James. They'd been frantic. They'd come back from Geneva early and reported me as missing to the police.

The bank had called my mother to ask if she was in Hong Kong, because if she wasn't she might want to know that someone was using her card to withdraw money from an ATM there. She informed the police, and had to tell them that if I was the one withdrawing Hong

Kong dollars, I hadn't exactly stolen her card, but I didn't exactly have permission to be flying around Asia with it either.

My parents didn't want to press charges against me for theft, or anything else for that matter. But once you report a problem to the police, it's not so easy to unreport it.

The police officer did a good job of scaring me out of my socks. I can't remember all the crimes he threw around, but unauthorized use of a credit card was one. Forgery was another. Some fancy terms for running away from home. A federal charge involving misuse of a passport. As he worked his way down the list, I started wondering who was going to be in prison longer, me or Ti-Anna's dad.

After convincing me that they were determined to send me to reform school, he sent me to talk to a juvenile court judge instead, not in a trial but in her office, in a kind of preliminary meeting.

She was scary too, in her way, but also interested in our story. She told me that, sadly and surprisingly, she comes across girls right here outside Washington, D.C., who have been sold into prostitution, not that different from the ones we saved from the truck. She hinted that if I kept paying my parents back, and did community service, and showed in my account of this whole thing that I'd learned a lesson, then maybe she'd let me stay with my family after all.

When I haven't been hand-packing pints of butter pecan, I've been writing this account, as she asked me to do. And I have given a lot of thought to her question about what lessons I learned.

I learned the best place to get dim sum in Hong Kong and pho bo in Hanoi, but I know that's not what she has in mind. I learned that when you use crutches, you should put as much weight as you can on your forearms. Otherwise your armpits will pay the price. But I don't think that's it, either.

I learned that once you start crossing a street in Hanoi, you shouldn't hesitate and you shouldn't turn back. Maybe I can convince her there's a life lesson in there somewhere.

I learned that there are people in the world you can trust, and people you can't trust, and it's not always easy to tell one from the other. Still, you can't let your fear of the second type keep you from taking chances, because the first type is a lot more common.

I'm afraid what I learned most of all sounds so obvious that the judge may wonder why I had to go halfway around the world to figure it out. That is, that not much in life is more important than friends.

Which brings me, one more time, to Ti-Anna.

Chapter 50

Since we've been back, we haven't been able to spend much time together. Her mother still doesn't think it's proper for her to come to my house or me to go to hers. When I'm not at work, I've been writing this essay. And with this stupid cast, I can't just bike over there when I have a few free minutes.

Still, we've talked.

When we got home we discovered that our press conference had made a bigger splash than we could have imagined, both because of the slave-trading ring we'd exposed and because of what we'd discovered about Ti-Anna's father. U.S. government officials had believed our story: you couldn't argue with the photos. People were shocked, or said they were, at how the Chinese had lured and kidnapped him.

The Vietnamese foreign ministry had demanded an explanation from China, and the American State Department had too, since Ti-Anna's dad is a legal U.S. resident. All the human rights groups had condemned what China had done.

The amazing part, according to Ti-Anna's father's friend at the

State Department, was that with so much coverage of the whole thing the Chinese government had felt compelled to respond. They put out a statement claiming that her dad was being held for illegally crossing the border from Vietnam into China.

"But that's ridiculous!" I sputtered into the phone when she was telling me all this.

"Of course," she said. "But still it's good news. First of all, they admitted that they're holding him. Now they won't let something terrible happen to him, or they'll get blamed.

"They haven't charged him with anything serious, like espionage or undermining the state," she continued. "If they leave it at crossing the border, they could let him go with a fine and not lose too much face. At least that's what our friend says."

"Let's hope so, for *their* sake," I said.

I could almost see Ti-Anna smiling on the other end of the phone. "Our next mission may be a little tougher without your mom's credit card," she said.

Some reporters called, but her mother and my parents agreed it would be better for us not to talk to them, and we were fine with that. Eventually our local weekly did a story about us, using a photo from the Hanoi press conference.

We each friended Wei right away. Getting her ID back a few hours late had been no big deal, she assured us. She had a great time in Hainan! She misses us!

We miss her too.

Ti-Anna promised to pay back half of what we'd spent, but so far her mother hasn't let her take a job. She's been busy helping her mom, as she told me when we finally got together this morning.

It's been one of those hot, still, late-July days, when you think a thunderstorm might be coming but you're not sure. I wasn't on the ice cream store schedule, and I wanted to uncramp my fingers and celebrate having almost finished this essay.

We met at the bike trail and walked together for a while. Ti-Anna didn't mind ambling at my broken-legged pace. When I told her I could use a rest, she was fine with that, too. We found a bench in the shade.

Ti-Anna was looking even prettier than usual. I thought it was because she seemed so happy and relaxed, and I told her so—not that she looked beautiful, of course, but that she seemed to be in good spirits.

She nodded.

"The best thing is how my mom seems to have bounced back," she told me. "She's applying for permission to visit my father, she's trying to hire a lawyer for him, she's talking to people about a petition campaign to free him."

"That's great," I said.

"And she told me: 'Ti-Anna, it was his decision to go back. We can try to help him, but he's responsible for his choices, like all of us.'"

"And that made you feel better," I suggested.

"I guess," she said. "It's funny, though. Now that I know he's alive and I can picture where he is, I've really been missing him."

"I get that," I said. "You didn't have time to miss him while we were looking."

Ti-Anna pulled two containers of rice and vegetables out of her shoulder bag, and two pairs of chopsticks.

"My mom made one for you," she said.

"You're kidding!" I took my sandwich out of my pocket. "Want this?"

"But then what will I do with mine?"

"You know," I said, "it takes a surprising number of calories to get around on crutches."

"I don't know why I even asked." She sighed and handed me both containers. "So am I going to get to read your masterpiece?"

225

I said yes, of course.

"I was going to go back, take out some of the embarrassing details, put in some good values the judge might like," I said. Since her mother had never reported her as missing, Ti-Anna wasn't having to deal with the judge like I was. "But I've decided not to change anything. After all, we were trying to do the right thing, right? What happened is what happened."

But when I offered to email it to her, she hesitated.

"Don't forget what Brian warned us," she said.

"I know," I said. "In fact, I think I might save them the trouble and put it all online. I figure there isn't much *they* don't know already. And since I'll have to admit at the end that there's nothing much more we can do for your father, I can't imagine there'll be anything in there to worry them."

"You will?" Ti-Anna said. "I mean, there's not?"

"Well, let's be honest, are we going to engineer a jailbreak fourteen thousand miles away in Kunming?"

Ti-Anna looked like she wanted to answer, but she didn't. I finished the first container and pushed the other one back to her.

"You know, on second thought, I'm kind of full," I said.

"You?" she said. "You're—" Then she stopped, and gave me one of her little half smiles. She slid the lunch back into her shoulder bag and put her hand on mine for a minute.

We stood up, surrounded by the buzz of the cicadas and the Washington warmth, and started back down the path.

Epilogue

Monday, July 30, 12:15 p.m. (EDT)

Beijing, China

It is past midnight, early Tuesday morning, and the man with the tie tucked into his shirt leans back. He drains the lukewarm remains of his fifth cup of tea and sighs.

He knows what he should do. He should send copies of this document to multiple offices for further analysis and after-action study. He should forward the name of this infernal boy to the border authorities, to make sure he stays on the watch list for entry into the country. He should set in motion the process to determine whether any of his subordinates, in Washington or Hong Kong or Hanoi, should be reprimanded or demoted.

But he does not want to do any of those things. What he wants is for the mess to go away. Oh, the original operation—the luring of the traitor back into custody—that went smoothly. But the botched operation with the daughter from the United States, and all the publicity afterward: a nightmare.

He barks to his young assistant, who is sitting outside his office wondering if she will go home at all tonight. He orders another cup of tea. It won't do his career any good to call more attention to this episode. And, really, is further analysis necessary? Everyone knows what went wrong. It is clear from the boy's rambling, overheated account that he is nothing but an amateur who stumbled into something he didn't understand. They won't be trying anything again soon, that much is clear. His document says so. And the girl will know better than to risk making things worse for her father.

At least the boy's leg is broken. There's some satisfaction in that.

His assistant brings tea on a small round tray, bows almost imperceptibly and retreats. When she has closed the door, he clips together the two printouts (English and Chinese), pulls open his bottom file cabinet drawer and drops the documents at the back. He blows on the tea, sips, leans back and pushes the drawer closed with his foot.

Rockville, Maryland

In her small windowless office, the juvenile court judge leans back in her chair, a half smile on her face. It's almost time for court, and the pile of orders and pleadings she had intended to plow through remains untouched on her desk. She doesn't mind.

The boy has taken her assignment seriously, and his personal account is a change of pace from her normal fare of child abuse, drugs and petty crime. She is pleased when she doesn't feel bound to inflict punishment. He did things he shouldn't have, no question, and she can't just let those slide. He made his parents frantic. He used their money. He forged their signatures.

He also saved those poor girls from a terrible life—more than she accomplishes, most days. He stood by a friend.

The judge thinks she can devise a community service plan that everyone will be happy with. Maybe he can teach kendo to some of my real troublemakers, she thinks. Once he gets out of his cast.

She leans forward and scrolls back to the final page, with Ethan's description of turning down a second lunch. Speaking in code indeed. She smiles, closes the attachment and tosses her empty coffee cup into the wastebasket. She steels herself for an afternoon in court.

Just outside Washington, D.C.

Seven miles to the south, the girl with the long black hair, striking eyebrows and sharp cheekbones leans back, smiling.

"What are you still doing on that computer, Ti-Anna?" her mother calls from the kitchen in Chinese. "Don't you want lunch?"

"One minute," she calls back.

Ti-Anna closes her eyes. The knocking of her air conditioner could almost be the waves slapping into the hull of the Hong Kong ferry. Seagulls drift along beside them, a rainbow dances through a spray of seawater. Ethan's arm is lightly around her shoulder. When the ferry docks, they will go through the gate, not over it.

"Ti-Anna!" her mother calls, more sharply.

She clicks the document closed.

"I'm coming," she answers.

Ethan's cast won't come off for a few more weeks, but soon enough he'll be riding his bike. They'll meet up when he gets off work, maybe. He'll wheel his bike as he walks her home.

She wonders what it will take to persuade her mother to let her spend time with an American boy. She's not sure. But she knows she will be working on it.

The Real Ti-Anna's Story

I was thirteen years old and living in Montreal when my father went missing. My name is Ti-Anna. The story you just read is a work of fiction, but many of the details and situations are based on truth. I will tell you the history this novel is based upon.

My father's name is Wang Bingzhang. He was a medical doctor from China who came to North America for graduate study in 1978. He was in awe of the civil liberties and democracy he found here. They were unknown in his homeland and were so inspiring that he gave up his career in medical research to found the overseas Chinese democracy movement. For twenty years, he worked unrelentingly to promote political change in China, until the struggle that had consumed his life cost him his freedom, too.

In 2002, my father went to northern Vietnam to meet with Chinese labor activists. When he left he told my mother and me that he would call us. Weeks passed and we didn't hear from him. I was not brave enough to go looking for him, but I remember my family's desperate attempts to get information on his whereabouts. We knew that he was considered an enemy of his own country because he was fighting for freedom. Six months passed before we finally learned that he had been kidnapped in Vietnam. He'd been forced into China and charged with planning to bomb the Chinese Embassy in Bangkok and spying for Taiwan. A trial was held in secret and he was sentenced to life in prison. When my mother told me what had happened, I was sure there had been a terrible mistake—that such injustice could not exist, and that if it did, it would not touch the sheltered life of a teenager like me living in North America.

My family pleaded with the governments of Canada, the United States and elsewhere to call for my father's release. In 2008, I put my education on hold for a year to advocate in Washington, D.C., for the government to help get my father's freedom.

Despite the international support we've been able to mobilize, my father continues to languish in prison. For ten years now, he has been in a tiny cell in Southern China. He is allowed one thirty-minute visit each month. My family takes turns making the journey from Vancouver, Montreal, New York City or Los Angeles, only to see him through layers of Plexiglas and prison bars. The mood is so heartbreaking, even the prison guards monitoring our visits have conveyed to us their sympathy.

It is true that I have traveled to meet questionable people in questionable places in the hope that I could understand my father's journey and ultimately win his freedom. Sometimes, my adventures have been rewarding, like the time my brother and I went looking for the Royal Thai Police colonel who investigated my father's supposed crimes. We traveled to Thailand with nothing but the colonel's name on a faded piece of paper. Luck led us to this man on the outskirts of Bangkok. When we met over tea and jackfruit, he exonerated my father of any wrongdoing. Over the years, I've also met many people, who, like some characters in this book, took a stand to help others. I know that like Sydney's, their heroic efforts to help complete strangers for the sake of a belief in humanity have changed lives for the better.

But the decade of my father's imprisonment has been marked largely by a sense of defeat and the helplessness one feels when confronting an adversary as formidable as the Chinese government. I don't have my father's idealism, eloquence or brazen ability to defy the Chinese communist regime. But I have always felt that if I cannot secure his release, at least I must ensure that his sacrifice is not in vain.

Often the challenges are overwhelming and my efforts seem meaningless, but I've come to realize that you can never know what may come from taking action—and you can be sure that nothing will come from sitting idle. Not everyone can be an effective public speaker or writer, but we all can make a difference in our own way. Ethan's eagerness to help is as important as Sydney's dedication.

However naive it may seem to believe that one individual can make a difference, the point is that we should not allow ourselves to be mere victims of adversity. With our rights come responsibilities to use whatever strengths we have and stand on the right side of history.

I think if my father knew that in exchange for his freedom, he had planted a seed for change in China, it would be a trade he would be willing to make many times over.

—Ti-Anna Wang

Author's Note

This story is fiction, but it's inspired by the type of stories I usually write—true ones.

I've spent most of my life working for a newspaper, the *Washington Post*, which has given me a chance to meet people like Sydney, Horace, Ti-Anna's father—and even a real Ti-Anna.

My first reporting from Asia didn't go well. I landed in Seoul, Korea, in 1987, just as thousands of university students were staging demonstrations against that country's military dictatorship.

Their story had a happy ending: Eventually, they were joined by thousands of other protesters, including many of their parents. The government agreed to hold free elections. South Korea evolved into what it is today: a prosperous, peaceful democracy.

But when I got there, things were confusing, and a little scary. Students with bandanas tied around their foreheads were heaving flaming Molotov cocktails into formations of riot police. Policemen, sweating inside padded green jackets and helmets, were firing tear gas back at the students.

On my first day, I made a true rookie mistake: I let myself get walloped in the leg by a tear-gas canister. I was lucky. If it had hit me in the chest or head, I would have really been in trouble. As it was, I got away with a welt, a lot of chemical-induced tears and a couple of useful lessons.

One was: Don't get stuck in no-man's-land between students throwing Molotov cocktails and riot police firing tear gas. You can write as good a newspaper article from behind one line or the other.

The other, which I learned slowly over the next weeks and months and years, was more important: people all over the world, in every country and every culture, want to live in freedom, and many of them will take amazing risks to get there. I saw evidence of that again in 1991, when the *Post* sent me and my wife (also a reporter) to Moscow to cover what turned out to be the collapse of the Soviet Union. I saw it in Indonesia in 1998, when ordinary people forced the dictator Suharto from power.

And in this century, while I've been running the *Post*'s editorial and opinion section in Washington, I've seen it in the eyes of brave people from all over the world: Egypt and Burma, Belarus and Zimbabwe, Cuba, Bahrain and, yes, China.

We call these people dissidents, or freedom fighters, or activists. They think of themselves as ordinary people who are tired of being pushed around—who want the same thing Thomas Jefferson wanted, which is to say, their "inalienable rights" of life, liberty and the pursuit of happiness.

Some of these freedom fighters come to the United States because they've been kicked out of their own countries. Some visit and then go back, even though they know they may be put in jail when they do.

Sometimes they come to Washington because they're hoping to convince Congress to appropriate money for their cause. Often they just want moral support. They want us to know that they're out there, fighting. They want us to appreciate our own freedom. And some come to the *Washington Post*, hoping we might write about their struggles.

That's how I met the real Ti-Anna, whose name is Ti-Anna Wang. When she came to Washington in 2008, she was older than the Ti-Anna in my story, but not by much. She had just graduated from high school.

Before starting college, she had decided to spend a year in Washington to bring attention to the case of her father, Wang Bingzhang, a founder of the overseas democracy movement who was by then in prison in China. We met for coffee in a hotel lobby across from the *Post* newsroom on 15th Street NW.

I was struck by her quiet determination, and asked her to write an article for the *Post*. Here's a snippet of what she wrote, in which she recounted what had happened to her father:

In June 2002, my father traveled to Vietnam to meet with two fellow labor activists. They were conferring over lunch in a restaurant near the China-Vietnam border when several men speaking Chinese ordered them into a car. Beaten, blindfolded and gagged, my father and his two colleagues were abducted into China by boat. They were left in a Buddhist temple in Guangxi Province for the Chinese authorities.

My father was held incommunicado for six months, in contravention of China's own Criminal Procedural Law, after which he was charged with "offenses of espionage" and the "conduct of terrorism." His "trial" lasted one day and was held behind closed doors. During the proceedings, my father was not allowed to speak, nor was any evidence presented or witnesses called. He was convicted and sentenced to life in prison. The identities of his abductors have never been discovered.

Ti-Anna succeeded in raising the profile of her father's case. Unfortunately, that wasn't enough to persuade China's government to let him go, even though his health has been declining in prison.

With her mother and her brother, Times Wang, she's still trying. Hopefully his release will come soon.

I didn't realize how much her story had stuck with me until I started writing this book the next summer. I thought it was going to be about a boy named Ethan, but before the second chapter had ended, a girl named Ti-Anna had made a quiet entrance. It turned into a book about both of them—and, though they never make it into mainland China, about China, too.

Like Ethan, I've been fascinated by China for a long time, though I've never lived there and I don't speak Chinese. I first visited China in 1977, when the country was just beginning to recover from the Cultural Revolution.

I remember the Beijing of 1977 as a poor, freezing city, wreathed in smoke and soot from coal fires. Everyone wore padded blue or gray jackets and walked or rode bicycles; only a few Party functionaries got to ride in cars.

For a visitor, it was magical, otherworldly, almost silent but for the bicycle bells. For residents, to an extent I couldn't appreciate at the time, it was a place of privation and fear. People dared not talk about how much they had suffered under the rule of Chairman Mao Zedong, who had died the year before.

By 2000, when I returned to interview President Jiang Zemin and see "the new China," Beijing was transformed. The city was still choking, but this time on automobile exhaust. There were gleaming new buildings. The Party was still in control, but it didn't try to run people's personal lives. People felt freer to talk—within limits.

As Ethan and the fictional Ti-Anna and their angry classmates in world history class could tell you, it's a complex story, and there's no single right way to view it. But what Ethan and Ti-Anna experience is certainly part of the story of modern China. According to Amnesty International, half a million people in China are in punitive detention, though they've never been charged with a crime or had a trial. The number of prisoners of conscience, like Wang Bingzhang, has been going up.

Modern-day slavery is not a product of my imagination either. Thousands of girls are tricked or taken from their homes and sold into prostitution, like the ones Ethan and Ti-Anna rescued from the truck. It happens everywhere, including in America, but it happens a lot more often in poor countries like Vietnam, Laos and Cambodia.

The good news is how many people, here in the United States and in those countries, are working to make things better. For readers who want to get involved, there's no need to head to faraway countries without telling your parents. There's a lot you can do.

There is an organization called International Justice Mission, which works with local police to promote the rule of law and help keep girls from being exploited. There are other groups that fight trafficking as well, including Free the Slaves, an organization dedicated to ending slavery worldwide, and Catholic Relief Services, the official humanitarian agency of the Catholic community in the United States. There is also MTV Exit, a campaign about freedom—our rights as human beings to choose where we live, where we work, who our friends are and who we love.

And there are organizations trying to promote, in a peaceful way, freedom and civil liberties in China, Vietnam and elsewhere: Human Rights Watch, China Human Rights Defenders, Human Rights in China and Amnesty International.

Acknowledgments

Thanks are owed to my discerning early readers, Pooh Shapiro and Joe Hiatt; my always supportive agent, Rafe Sagalyn; my wise and talented editor, Beverly Horowitz; and above all my loving and encouraging family: Pooh, Joe, Alex Hiatt and Nate Hiatt. I also am grateful to Ti-Anna Wang for what she taught me, and to the many dissidents and freedom fighters around the world who have been willing to share their stories.

About the Author

Fred Hiatt is the editorial page editor and a columnist for the *Washington Post*, where he began working in 1981. He and his wife served as co–bureau chiefs of the *Post*'s Northeast Asia Bureau in Tokyo, reporting on Korea and Japan. They then served as correspondents and co–bureau chiefs in Moscow. Before joining the *Post*'s foreign staff, Hiatt covered U.S. military and national security affairs. He also worked as a reporter for the *Atlanta Journal* and the *Washington Star* in Washington, D.C., and wrote for the *Harvard Crimson*. He is the author of two books for young readers, *If I Were Queen of the World* and *Baby Talk*, and the adult novel *The Secret Sun*. Fred Hiatt and his wife have three children and live in Maryland.